JILL FOR JULIA

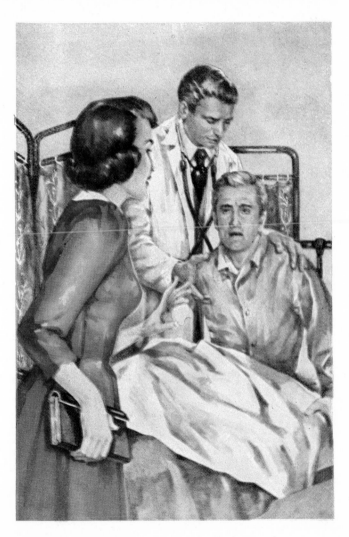

She tried to speak, but the words would not come

EDITH MILES

JILL FOR JULIA

FANFARE
SERIES

SPRING BOOKS · LONDON

Published by

SPRING BOOKS

SPRING HOUSE · SPRING PLACE · LONDON NW 5

Printed in Czechoslovakia

T 431

CONTENTS

LIST OF ILLUSTRATIONS

CHAPTER I

AN OLD HEAD ON YOUNG SHOULDERS

'So it's you, Julie, that has to go chasing through the brook after Frisky, while Em'line plays her piano, and your brother goes off on the back of somebody's motor-bike!' said old Betty as she looked at the soaked footwear of her master's second daughter; 'and you with that cold still about you!'

Jill, as she was called by the family, held up a warning finger. 'Do be a darling, Betty,' she said in an urgent whisper, 'and keep this quiet. If I change my shoes and stockings out here, no one need know. I particularly don't want Daddy disturbed this afternoon.'

Old Betty pointed to the fireside. 'Sit you there, Julie,' she said, 'I'll get your other shoes and some dry stockings. I'd not run round for either of the others, but I don't mind

doing it for you, seeing that you are always
so willing to give me a hand.'

She tossed a towel across to the girl as she
spoke, and Jill thankfully caught it, and
stripping off her wet shoes and stockings,
rubbed her feet briskly as she held them to
the comforting warmth of the kitchen range.
It was a cold spring day, and her chase after
the pony, though quite exciting while it lasted,
had distinctly uncomfortable results.

'Thanks so much, Betty,' said Jill, when
the old housekeeper came back. 'Now I shall
be all right, and I can go and shut up the
hens. I was on my way to do that when I saw
that Frisky was breaking bounds again.'

'You'll do nothing of the sort, Julie,' said
the old woman. 'You'll sit there and drink
a good hot cup of tea. I'm going to make it
this minute, and you can leave the fowls to
me. You've been on the run since six this
morning, and you should have had at least
a couple of days in bed.'

'You were up at five,' said Jill, but the old

woman did not answer. She made the tea, brought cups, milk and sugar, and poured out for Jill.

'I like mine to brew a bit,' she said. 'It'll be just right if I leave it on the hob while I go to the hen house.'

She was off before Jill had taken her first sip.

'Dear old Betty!' thought the girl. 'What should we have done without her all these years? The others think she is surly, but I don't! Her plain speaking is good for us, anyhow!'

Jill poked the fire thoughtfully. 'She's right as usual. I shall have to slow up a bit, for things have been so rushed that I've hardly time to think nowadays, and I *must* get my thoughts in order before Great Aunt Julia comes to-morrow.'

Miss Julia Lomax was a formidable old lady who paid periodic visits to the farm, and told her relatives just what she thought of them. Even old Betty's candour was nothing beside that of Great Aunt Julia. Jill had been named after her, but the rest of the family flatly refused to use the dreaded name when addressing her, and on old Betty's tongue it was softened to 'Julie' and uttered with a tenderness which the old woman showed to no other member of the family, not even to Gwen, the youngest of the Lomaxes, though Gwen was certainly second in old Betty's favour.

'Now how can I put it to her?' mused Jill. 'I hate asking favours of any one, most of all I hate asking them of Great Aunt Julia, and Gwen is the only person for whose sake I would do such a thing. But Gwen *shall* go to college, if I have to sing in the streets to get the money for her fees! I'd be sure of heaps of pennies to go in the next street!'

Jill giggled a little nervously at the idea, and then gave herself a little shake. This wasn't getting her thoughts in order! It was just being silly. 'Is this cold making me light-headed?' she asked herself. 'After all, Great

Aunt Julia is our nearest relative, and it's the first time I've ever asked her to do anything for us. Then, Gwen is determined to pay back the money for her training as soon as she starts earning, so it won't be such a tremendous favour, after all. Gwen will make such a splendid teacher, it would be a shame if she couldn't get her training after doing so well at High School. It's not as if there was no one else to look after Dad and keep things running as smoothly as possible here.'

Jill could not repress a sigh at this point, for when she had left school two years earlier, she had been full of plans for herself. She wanted to be a nurse, and indeed, she had become one during the first weeks of the holiday which followed her school days, for her father had met with a serious accident and had been in bed for many months. He was able to get up now, but he had by no means fully recovered, and as Jill had taken charge of things during his illness, he allowed her to go on seeing to his affairs.

She had not been without help, of course.
Old Betty was a tower of strength, and worth
her weight in gold. Freddie, Jill's senior by
eighteen months or so, considered that *he* was
running the farm, of course, but in practice,
it was Jill who made decisions, wrote letters,
gave orders to the men, and did all the
worrying. As for Emmeline, she contributed
but little to the well-being of the household.
She was inclined to resent old Betty's free
and easy ways, and to stand on her dignity
as the eldest daughter, mistress of the house,
and so on, and Jill was often sadly put to it
to keep the peace between them. Emmeline
sighed for elegances which did not fit in with
old Betty's homely notions. Betty thought
Emmeline lazy as well as affected, and Jill
kept them apart as much as she could, trying
tactfully to make Emmeline see that old
Betty was far too valuable to the household
for them to risk offending her, especially
while Mr. Lomax was ill and money so
hard to come by.

'I know!' said Jill, brightening under the warmth of the fire and the stimulation of old Betty's cup of tea, 'I'll put it to Great Aunt Julia that this expense for Gwen will really be an investment — we'll keep it on a business footing and all that!'

She gave a start of surprise as a hand was placed on her shoulder. 'Why, Great Aunt Julia!' she said, 'we weren't expecting you till to-morrow. I'm so sorry that no one went to meet you!'

Meeting Great Aunt Julia with the pony trap was a sort of family function, to be carried out with all due solemnity.

'I'm not such a fool as to expect to be met when no one knew I was coming,' said the old lady, looking at her nephew's daughter with shrewd but by no means unkindly eyes. 'Your letter showed you were worrying about something, Julia, so I decided to come as soon as I could and give you the benefit of my advice.'

'Thank you,' said Jill, a little faintly. 'It's

now or never!' she thought. 'I shan't get such a good opening again.'

She sprang up to bring a chair for the old lady, who had already discarded her outdoor clothing. 'Yes, I did want to talk to you,' she said. 'I can't worry Dad now, and I know you are always so ready to advise us. It's about Gwen,' she went on quickly, not daring to pause lest she should find herself unable to restart. 'She so wants to go to a teachers' training college—she'll make a wonderful teacher, I'm sure, but with Dad's illness and one thing and another, I'm worried about how we are to find the money. Gwen will pay it back when she's earning, of course, but in the meantime——'

'In the meantime you can leave all that to me!' said Great Aunt Julia. 'Is that all you were worrying about, child? Queer that you should bother yourself with such a trifle! I thought your father was worse, or that Freddie had done something stupid, or that Emmeline was being a sillier doll than usual, or that old

Betty couldn't stand her tantrums any longer! If Betty left now, that would be something to fret over, I'll admit!'

'It would indeed,' said Jill. 'Thanks so much, Great Aunt Julia! You've no idea what a load it is off my mind to think that dear old Gwen will have her heart's desire.'

'And what about you?' said the old lady somewhat grimly.

'Oh, I stay here, and do odd jobs and so forth,' said Jill lightly.

'Let Jill do it, eh?' retorted the old lady. 'I've heard that said a good many times in this house, haven't I? A sort of family motto, I suppose.'

'Well, even a stop-gap is a little use sometimes,' said Jill. 'I won't offer you a cup of Betty's tea, because I know you'd rather wait till five o'clock. Shall we go and find Gwen, and tell her the glad tidings?'

'You go,' said Great Aunt Julia, 'I'll have a word with your father.'

Jill smiled her thanks and sped off to her

sister, who was in their bedroom putting away some clothing.

'It's all absolutely fixed, my Gwen!' she cried rapturously. 'Great Aunt Julia is a sport, and she's going to see things through for you! I could thank her on my bended knee! Why, my blessed baby!' she added, as her sister slipped down to the floor, and clutched at her knees, 'what do you think you are doing?'

'I'm thanking *you* on my bended knees, Jill,' sobbed Gwen. 'You're just marvellous. No one else would have done this for me. I'd never have dared to do it for myself. You know how nervous Great Aunt Julia makes me!'

'That must change, my infant,' said Jill, setting her sister on her feet again. 'She's not the dragon we've always thought her. She's a brick with a heart of gold!'

They both laughed at the phrase.

'A lovely mixed metaphor!' said Gwen. 'I'll save it up for my exam. papers!' She faltered and said, wistfully, 'If only you were coming too, Jill!'

'But you know I'm not half clever enough for teaching,' said Jill. 'I'm just a blundering, impetuous, harum-scarum creature fit for nothing but odd jobs. Being so odd myself, I'm just suited for them!'

'You're the best sister in the world,' said Gwen; 'come and help me thank Great Aunt Julia if I'm not to be allowed to tell you all I think about you!'

CHAPTER II

JILL MEETS A STRANGER

Gwen went off to college in September, divided between interest in the new life, and regret at leaving the old one. Miss Lomax had chosen a London college for her, and meant to see as much of the girl as possible.

'I'll write every week, Jill, and tell you all about everything,' said Gwen when they parted.

'Don't work too hard, kiddie,' said Jill, who had snatched an hour to see her off. 'I'll keep you well informed about home affairs, but our humdrum ways will be very tame beside your merry doings.'

'I shall love every word you write,' said Gwen with a little lump in her throat, 'and I shall just *ache* for Christmas.'

Jill had ached, too, for the girl's departure

18

would leave a blank that all her other interests could not fill. She set aside Sunday evenings for writing to Gwen, who read and re-read every letter avidly, and was kept in touch with home by their vivid detail and humorous touches.

Gwen's own letters contained long descriptions of her new life, and her hasty visits to Aunt Julia. She soon settled down and was quite happy, though she missed Jill very much at first. Jill lived for her letters, and watched for the postman every Wednesday morning.

The Christmas holidays were all too short for the amount of talking that the two girls had to do. Gwen had grown up in the course of that one term, and had left the schoolgirl very far behind. She was now almost as independent as Jill herself, and Jill was delighted with her.

'You make me feel quite young and ignorant,' she said. 'You are so self-possessed—quite an air with you, I declare!'

'That's rot!' said Gwen. 'I feel a mere

baby—as if I ought to bring a little stool, and sit down at your feet.'

Jill laughingly set a stool on the rug for her, and Gwen sat on it, with her arm resting on Jill's knee.

'I love college,' she said, 'but it's heavenly to come home again. I'm glad Great Aunt Julia didn't press me to go to her for Christmas after all.'

'She asked me, too,' said Jill.

'I didn't know that,' said Gwen, starting with surprise. 'Why, I'd have gone like a shot if you had been there, Jill.'

'How could I go?' asked Jill, glancing at the opposite side of the fire, where her father sat dozing.

Gwen did not answer, and soon Mr. Lomax roused and wanted to hear more about the life at college.

Holding Jill's hand in hers, Gwen rattled on merrily, telling little incidents and jokes and taking care that Jill was not drawn into the conversation, for the strong brown hand

'I love college,' she said, *'but it's heavenly to come home again'*

was trembling, and Gwen caught the sound of more than one sigh.

Jill found it hard to lose Gwen after the holidays. 'It's lonelier than ever!' she sighed as she stood by the gate one evening after tea. Jill hated the dark evenings, and found the winter days all too short for the many things she had to do out of doors.

The weeks slipped by quicker than she had expected, however, and she was able to count off the days to Easter more cheerfully as the interval grew shorter. She had much to plan and contrive, for she did not want Gwen to realize how badly things were going.

That they were going badly Jill could not deny, for in spite of all her efforts, fate had been against them. Stock had died, accidents had happened, and altogether things looked blacker than at any time since her father's illness.

The afternoon post had brought her a letter from Gwen, and she took it out to read as she strolled through the fields to look at a gate that wanted mending. A beautiful spring day had carried her thoughts back to the old carefree times, and she felt that she wanted to be alone for a while.

She walked on to the lane which led to the station, and stood leaning on the stile there. Even the peacefulness of the spring evening, with its promise of summer days to follow, could not smooth the wrinkles from Jill's forehead.

Her mind was running on the cares which the others left her to deal with as a matter of course.

'Two new gates—that old one can't be mended any more—and the wagon wants a new wheel. Then if we don't replace Dapple, the feed will be wasted—why *did* Freddy forget that insurance money? We could have got another cow as a matter of course with the compensation.'

Her reverie was interrupted by the sight of a stranger, who had just turned the corner of the lane. Jill could see at once that he was what Betty called an 'outcomer' and that he was new to the neighbourhood.

'A tourist, I should think! It's early for them, though. That hat was never bought in an English shop. His shoes, too, look at those blocked toes!'

She had dropped her eyes to avoid meeting those of the passer-by, and when he had gone, she gave herself a little shake of reproof.

'Staring at a man's shoes and making remarks to yourself when you have plenty of your own business to think about!' she said. 'What you have to do is to find some means of raking up a hundred pounds. A hundred pounds,' she repeated, forming the words with her lips by way of emphasis, as if to impress the enormity of the sum upon her brain.

A shadow made her look up, and she saw that the man who had passed had turned round, and was coming back as if to speak to her.

She waited till he came within a few feet, and his long shadow was reaching past her into the field. Then she looked at him frankly. 'Did you want to ask me something?' she said.

If he had any other motive for turning back than merely to ask his way, he thought better of it, and hid his change of front very skilfully.

'I had a direction to the village,' he said, 'but I was afraid I might have missed the track. This doesn't look as if it went anywhere in particular.'

'It's right for the village,' said Jill, a little sharply. 'Half a mile or so, and straight on. You can't miss it.'

She turned away as she spoke, by way of hinting that she had not the least intention of prolonging the conversation.

The stranger raised his hat, and thanked her.

With a curt 'Good evening' Jill went away by the field path. It ran close under the hedge, and she could just see the top of the man's hat as he walked along the lane.

'Ridiculous to be walking along like this,' said Jill. 'He'll think I am doing it on purpose.

I'll strike across the field, and get back to the path later on. He's not to know that the path follows the lane.'

Just as she left the path, she heard a dull thud, and saw a small packet lying a few yards from the hedge.

'Who threw that over?' she thought. 'I wonder if I ought to pick it up.'

As she stood hesitating, the wind fluttered the packet slightly, and she took it up, with a suspicion that it was not just discarded paper which had been thrown away, but something of value, for she could see some fine black lines written in copper plate.

'Banknotes!' said Jill, counting them rapidly, 'banknotes for a hundred pounds!'

CHAPTER III

A HUNDRED POUNDS

Jill stood looking at the notes, and wondering what she ought to do. She did not at first connect them with the stranger who had spoken to her at the stile, but after a time she realized that he must have thrown them over the hedge.

She had quick ears, and she was sure that no one else had been passing at the time. As soon as she had recovered from her surprise, she hurried back to the stile, as that was the quickest way of getting into the lane, and ran towards the village, hoping to overtake him before he left the road and entered one of the inns. She did not want to excite comment by asking for him in the village.

But she soon found that he had not gone to the village at all. She asked the children playing on the green if they had seen a strange gentleman, but they were all very sure that no stranger had come to the village.

Visitors were rare in Littlemore, and always came in for a good deal of curious attention. Jill felt sure that the man could not have come there without being seen. She was equally sure that he could not have had time to turn back to the station before she reached the stile. Then where was he, and how was she to restore the packet that he must have tossed away by mistake?

Here was another problem for Jill. She saw no way out of it, for she could not be sure of knowing the man if she saw him again after an interval. To publish her find might invite false claims which she would have difficulty in refuting. Yet how could she keep this money which had fallen at her feet in so strange a manner?

'It's tantalizing,' she said, 'just the sum that I was thinking we wanted to tide us over our difficulties, too. Well, I suppose I had

better say nothing about it for a time, but
wait and see if any inquiries are made. I will
lock it away, and keep it from the others.'

She tucked the money into the front of her
dress, and went home. She had business
letters to write before dark, and she was later
than she had meant to be on account of her
search for the tourist.

She was surprised to find that her father
was not alone. Seated on the opposite side of
the fire was a tall man, whom she seemed to
remember slightly, though she could not recol-
lect for the moment where she had seen him.
The firelight flickering on his face did not
give her the chance of any close scrutiny, and
she turned to her father to say, 'I beg your
pardon, Dad, I did not know you were en-
gaged.'

'Don't run away, Jill,' said Mr. Lomax, 'I
was hoping you would come in soon. Allow
me to introduce a cousin, Mr. Cyrus J. Lomax, from America.'

'I'm delighted to see you, Cousin Jill,'

said a voice which made her start. 'I've taken the liberty of looking in for I've precious few relatives on either side the pond, and have to make the most of those I can trace.'

Jill's heart pounded strangely. 'I'm pleased to meet you,' she said formally. She realized that this was the stranger she had been looking for in the village—the owner of the notes!

'What do you think of her for a Lomax?' asked her father. 'Great Aunt Julia always declares that Jill's more of a Lomax than I am!'

The visitor seemed glad of a chance of looking at her and Jill felt as if his critical gaze must be spying the little bulge in her dress that showed where the notes lay hidden.

'She sure is a dandy girl,' he said frankly. 'I guess that she is some farmer, too.'

'She's just splendid,' said Mr. Lomax, 'she has kept things going since I have been ill. She must be a better farmer than I ever was, by this time. Fetch the others, Jill, will you?

And hurry supper, my dear, Mr. Lomax will be hungry after his journey.'

'Say now, you mustn't take that trouble. I ordered supper and bed at the station hotel. I'll stroll back along that little footpath they called the road when I've had the pleasure of seeing my other cousins.'

'I can't hear of that!' cried Mr. Lomax. 'You must stay with us while you are in this part of the country.'

The American cousin made some half-hearted protests, but Jill could see that he was pleased with the idea. She went out hastily to find Freddie and Emmeline, and after sending them to her father, went to tell Betty about the visitor, and ask her to get supper at once.

'I'll see to the bedroom,' she said. 'We'll put him in the one next to the porch. Don't you bother to come up, Betty.'

She had made up her mind what to do with the money, and when she had made up the bed, she slipped the packet, just as it was, under the edge of the pillow, where it would be hidden when she put the sheets and blankets back in position, but where it could not fail to attract the attention of the occupant of the bed.

Then with a lighter heart she set out towels, fetched water and soap, and after giving a final glance to make sure that all was in perfect order, she went down to the dining-room.

Any lingering doubts she had had were banished by the look of recognition that the American cousin gave her as he saw her in the circle of lamplight. But he made no reference to having seen her before, and Jill herself was not sufficiently at her ease to do so. She was glad that Emmeline did most of the talking, and so left her in the background where she quietly lessened old Betty's tasks as much as she could.

It was very interesting to listen to the cousin's conversation. He had travelled on the Continent, and was used to mixing with all sorts of people. His self-confidence was tempered by a pleasing modesty, and his frank and charming smile made his hearers quite at home with him. Jill had to admit that only her anxiety about the banknote incident kept her from enjoying the evening.

'I hope he stays long enough to see Gwen,' she thought. 'Gwen would love to hear him talk. What a lot he has seen! It will do father good to have his company.'

She looked across at Mr. Lomax who had forsaken his usual chair by the fire to preside at the supper table in honour of the visitor. His face was full of interest, and he looked more alert than Jill had seen him look since the accident.

The conversation turned to the subject of relatives.

'You must go and see Great Aunt Julia,' said Mr. Lomax, 'she will be delighted to be able to trace another branch of the family.'

'Say now, I like the sound of her,' said Cyrus J. 'I hope her welcome will be as warm as yours. Where does she live?'

'In Bloomsbury,' said Mr. Lomax. 'You know the district, I expect.'

'I do that, sir. British Museum, eh? I must get you to give me her address, and I'll write to her.'

'Jill is writing to-night or to-morrow,' said Mr. Lomax. 'She will introduce you, so to speak. I am afraid I must leave you in the hands of the young people now, as I am still an invalid, and keep early hours.'

Mr. Lomax went off upstairs, followed by Jill, who always saw him settled for the night. She did not go back to the dining-room again until her own bed-time, when she asked Freddie to show the visitor to his room.

CHAPTER IV

CONCERNING CYRUS J.

Jill went to bed but she could not sleep for thinking of the incident in the lane.

'Was it a mistake?' she asked herself, 'or did he *mean* to throw that money over the hedge for me to find? It seems impossible, for he didn't even know I was his cousin then. And I'm sure I wasn't talking out loud. He can't be a thought-reader! Yet—the very sum I was thinking of! Not that we could take it from him. And I was making up my mind to ask Great Aunt Julia to lend it to us, too. She said she would help. I don't mind asking her—at least not very much, for she will know that I have done my best, and all farmers get a spell of bad luck sometimes.'

The clock struck eleven, and reminded her that she ought to be asleep.

'I must write to Great Aunt Julia before breakfast,' she thought, 'I couldn't very well do it last night. I do wish he had kept that money in his pocket. Just spoilt his visit for me, having that packet in my frock when I was introduced to him. I like to hear him talk. His accent isn't very noticeable unless he gets excited.'

She went to sleep at last, but her dreams were haunted by a packet of banknotes which she was very anxious to get rid of, but which kept turning up in all sorts of unlikely places. But she woke at the usual time, and was busy milking when the American cousin came into the yard.

'Good morning, Mr. Lomax,' she said shyly, still thinking of the notes. She felt sure from the way in which he looked at her that he had found the packet under his pillow.

'Say "Cousin Cyrus",' he commanded. 'I'm going to call you Cousin Jill, if you don't mind.'

'That's all right,' said Jill. 'Call me what you like, Mr. — I mean, Cousin.'

'I was thinking I'd write a line to Great Aunt Julia and say I'd be glad to know when I could call on her.'

'I've just finished,' said Jill, picking up her pail, 'I'll find some notepaper for you, and give you the address.'

Cyrus J. took the pail from her and carried it into the dairy. Then Jill led the way to the hall.

'There's a little writing-table in the room next to yours,' she said, 'perhaps you'd like to use that while you are here. It's very quiet there; no one uses the room now that Gwen is at college.'

'It's a jolly little room,' he said, when Jill opened the door, 'over the porch, isn't it?'

'Yes,' said Jill, 'Gwen and I used to do our home lessons here, and read story-books on wet days.'

'I'll be glad to sit here to read and write,' said the cousin, 'but you mustn't let me turn you out. Come here just as usual, won't you?'

'I—I don't get much time for reading now,'

faltered Jill. Something in the way he was looking at her brought back the embarrassment of last night.

'But these are your books,' said Cousin Cyrus, going to the little shelves and taking down volume after volume. He patted the covers with the touch which only a book-lover can give, and seemed to recognize some old friends.

'The notepaper is in the table drawer,' said Jill, turning to go.

'Wait a bit, Cousin Jill,' was the reply. Her visitor slipped over to the door, and stood with his back against it. 'I've got something that belongs to you.'

He held out the bundle of notes as he spoke.

Jill flushed and looked at him reproachfully.

'You ought to know that I couldn't think of taking them,' she said.

'Why not?'

Jill found it rather hard to explain, so she took refuge in a question.

'Why did you throw them over the hedge?'
she asked.

'How do you know that I threw them?' he
answered with a smile.

'Because if you had known nothing about
them in the first place, you wouldn't be talking
to me about them now. You would have
spoken to Father about finding them.'

'One to you, Cousin Jill!' said Cyrus cheerfully. 'Well, let me explain. I've put in a lot
of time in a noisy factory, where it is impossible to hear oneself speak, much less hear
what any one else says to you; so I've picked
up a little lip-reading — got quite good at it, in
fact. Well, you picture me, Cousin Jill, full
of delight at finding this quaint little corner
of old England; bucked at the idea of meeting
some cousins. I walk down a lane and see
a girl muttering to herself and frowning
something dreadful.'

'Was I?' said Jill, in surprise.

'You sure were, cousin. I think as I pass,
"She's too young to be so worried, poor child;" '

'I'm not quite a baby,' Jill reminded him.

'I turn back with some fool question about the way, which I knew perfectly well, to see if I can find out what's troubling the child, and I see on her lips, "A hundred pounds!"'

Jill looked more surprised than ever.

'I find she is not the least bit inclined to have a friendly chat with a stranger, so I have to go on without asking her what's the matter. But see now, I've a good supply of ready cash with me, and think that a bit of it would be well spent in taking the creases out of that forehead.'

'Do you usually throw your money about like this?' said Jill, half laughing in spite of her annoyance.

'An exceptional case! Guess I must have felt the relationship without knowing it! Now be a sport, Cousin Jill; put those notes away, and say no more about it. You are not taking them from a stranger, you know.'

'But I can't!' said Jill. 'It's impossible. What would the others say?'

'Tell 'em you picked the wretched things up—that will be perfectly true,' said Cyrus, who was now growing uncomfortable.

'I should at once be told to take them to the police,' said Jill. 'Look here, cousin, I'll be frank with you. We do want money for the farm, but Great Aunt Julia will lend us some for a few months. I was just making up my mind to ask her when you came along.'

'Then why the frown?' asked Cyrus promptly.

'Because I had been vain enough to think that I could do everything off my own bat, and I didn't like having to admit to myself that I had failed.'

'I don't believe it was your fault,' said Cyrus stoutly.

'Well, perhaps I was not much to blame,' said Jill. 'I've done my best since father's accident, and Great Aunt Julia knows it. I needn't mind telling her how we stand.'

Cyrus took out his pocket-book and put the notes away. Then he looked at Jill, who faced him frankly now that she had gained her point.

'Cousin Jill,' he said, 'I want to be your pal. You're the right sort, and I've too good an opinion of you to do anything you don't approve of. But I want to make a bargain with you. If the time ever comes when I can do you a service, will you tell me so, without any reserve?'

Jill held out her brown hand.

'I will, Cousin Cyrus,' she said.

'Good,' said Cyrus, giving her hand a hearty grip. 'Now that note business is done with. We won't refer to that again. I was a clumsy fool, but I know you've forgiven me, by the way you agree to our bargain.'

'You're very good,' said Jill. 'I've nothing to forgive really, you know. And I'm very glad you have come to see us. Here's Great Aunt Julia's address. I'm sure you will like her. She's been a brick to Gwen and me.'

'I'm going to like this cousin,' said Jill to herself as she went downstairs. 'He's so sensible.'

'There's grit and pluck for you!' thought Cyrus J. as the door closed behind Jill. 'Didn't she just stand up to me? I guess she knows her own mind, and is not so easily got over as some of them! I must see more of her than I did last night. She was kind of keeping out of the way then, I guess.'

Mr. Lomax came down to breakfast in rare good spirits. He offered to show his cousin round the farm. Jill could hardly believe her ears, for he had not set foot in the yard even, since his accident.

'You won't over-tire yourself, Father?' she said a little timidly. Mr. Lomax smiled at the concern in her voice.

'You see how I am tyrannized over by my daughter,' he said to Cyrus with a laugh. 'You shall come with us, Jill, and take care of me. Then Cousin Cyrus can have first-hand information about English farming.'

Cyrus seemed very pleased with the suggestion.

'I've not farmed myself,' he said, 'having

lived in the city, and put in most of my time in the factory and office. But I love the look of these dandy little English fields, and I shall be glad to go round with you and Cousin Jill.'

Jill was better pleased with the idea than she would have been before she had had her frank talk with the visitor, and after breakfast the three set out.

'Jill, you have done wonders,' said her father. 'Why, child, you must have worked like a horse. I know very well that most of this is your doing. I never realized that so much was falling on your shoulders.'

'I've tried to keep things going,' said the girl. 'Of course, Freddie has helped, and some of the neighbours have given me good advice from time to time.'

When they reached the far end of the farm, Mr. Lomax rested on a stile, while Jill went to speak to one of the farm-hands who was working a little way off.

'I am afraid I have been very neglectful of my duty,' said Mr. Lomax, to his cousin. 'I

was so weak after my accident that I left Jill
to run the farm.'

'I guess you couldn't have had a better
manager!' said Cousin Cyrus, looking at Jill
with frank and obvious admiration, as she
returned from her errand.

'She did so well, and took such pains to
spare me all anxiety, that I am afraid I have
let her overwork. But she shall be relieved of
some of the responsibility now. I feel after
going round the fields once more that I want
to be back at work.' The last words were
overheard by his daughter, but Jill could
hardly believe her ears.

'But, Dad,' she said, 'hadn't you better see
Dr. Wilson before you start again?'

'I know what his sentiments are, Jill. He
as good as told me to sit still as long as I
could. Well, I am not content to sit still, any
longer.'

'I shall have to see that you don't do too
much at first, I can see!' said Jill. 'You are
not strong enough to be out for long at a time.'

'Isn't she a tyrant, Cyrus?' said Mr. Lomax. 'She rules us with a rod of iron. Take care that the worms don't turn, Jill! I'm beginning to feel rebellious.'

'Don't you take any notice of him, Jill,' said her cousin. 'He's lucky to have such a boss, and he knows it. I'll take your part, don't you fear!'

'Jill doesn't need a champion,' laughed Mr. Lomax, 'and she doesn't like folk to interfere when she has a job in hand. I tried to help her put the door on her doll's house once — a very long time ago, as you can imagine, for she gave up all such things when she was still quite small. I have never forgotten how my offer was met.'

'I'm sure,' Jill broke in, 'that Cousin Cyrus is not the least bit interested.'

'Oh, but I am! Do tell me, sir.'

'She said, "Don't *you* come bovvering when I'm busy!"' said Mr. Lomax with a smile. 'Now what do you think of that for six years old?'

'Showed plenty of independence, if the gratitude was missing,' said Cyrus, 'but I expect she did the job all right, didn't she?'

'Oh, yes, quite creditably. I must take you on to the barns, Cyrus, I should like your opinion about one of our reapers.'

The talk turned to farm matters again, and Jill was silent. She meant to see the doctor that afternoon, and find what he thought about her father's sudden renewal of interest in the farm.

Dr. Wilson listened intently to all Jill told him. His face reassured her before he spoke.

'This cousin came just at the right moment,' he said. 'Your father was ready to get out again, you see, but the impetus was lacking. When he wanted to show the American cousin the farm, his old interest came back. No doubt he realizes that he and you will be sharing the responsibility, and he is ready, and even eager to resume work under those conditions.'

'And work won't hurt him?' asked Jill.

'Certainly not! He mustn't overdo it at first, of course, but I can trust you to see to that. I'm glad that your chief worry is lifted from your shoulders, capable as they are, for you have had to much to do since your father's accident.'

'Will he get quite well now?'

'I see no reason why he shouldn't. Physically he is quite fit, so far as I can judge. He will probably be able to do as much work as ever he did.'

'Then I could be spared,' said Jill, half to herself.

'Why do you want to be spared?' said the doctor.

'I meant to be a nurse, but the accident happened just after I left school, and of course, I couldn't leave home then.'

'You won't be able to think of leaving for some time to come, my dear. Your father will still look to you a great deal, I feel sure. I will make a point of seeing him within the next few days. I am delighted that he has turned the corner. The lethargy which follows a bad illness is often more difficult to deal with than the illness itself. You can't hurry matters in the least with such a case.'

'No escape for me yet,' thought Jill, as she cycled home. 'But what a pig I am, to be groaning about that, when I ought to be rejoicing that Dad is almost himself again.'

CHAPTER V

FAMILY AFFAIRS

Great Aunt Julia sent prompt replies to the letters which Jill and Cyrus had written to her.

Jill's was short. It ran:

'Cheque enclosed. Why didn't you ask before? I shall come with Gwen for the Easter holidays.'

Jill showed it to her father, for they had been going over the farm accounts during the last two days. Mr. Lomax was keen to know about everything that Jill had done, and he was able to assure her that he had money in reserve which might have been used. Without appealing to any one, but just by mentioning the matter to her father, Jill could have replaced the stock, had repairs carried out, and then had a little money in hand.

'I don't know what to think,' said Jill to herself when she made this discovery. 'Of course, I couldn't have bothered Dad three days ago. I should have been afraid to upset him. Now am I glad or sorry that Cousin Cyrus caught me muttering in the lane? It showed me what a good sort he is, though it was embarrassing to have to make him take that money back.'

She went up to the little writing-room over the porch, for she wanted to tell the American cousin that Great Aunt Julia was coming to the farm.

'I'll tell him about the money, too,' she thought, 'I think he will be glad to know.'

She tapped on the door, and entered when the friendly voice called, 'Come in!'

'Say now,' he added, as he saw his caller, 'I thought it was that dear old soul Betty, come to bring me a little snack of "summat" so that I shouldn't faint before breakfast. Fancy *your* knocking, Cousin Jill, when you know that I only use this room on condition

that you don't come here any the less when
I am in it.'

Jill avoided a discussion on this point by
telling the object of her visit at once. 'I've
heard from Great Aunt Julia,' she said. 'She's
coming for Easter.'

'Yes, I made that much out from what she
wrote me,' said Cyrus, ruffling his hair, and
giving a perplexed glance at the letter which
he held in his hand.

'She sent the money,' said Jill, dropping
into a confidential tone, 'and wanted to know
why I didn't ask her before.'

'Good for Great Aunt Julia!' said Cyrus
approvingly, 'though it does me out of a
chance—but enough of that!'

'I needn't have asked her, really,' said Jill,
'for when Dad and I went through the
accounts, we found that he had enough by
him to meet the extra expenses.'

'I wish you would read this out to me,
Cousin Jill,' said Cyrus, holding out his letter.
'It doesn't seem to convey much to me yet.

But if you read it slowly—very slowly, mind—it may sink in!'

Jill could not wholly suppress the chuckle which this appeal drew from her, for though she had grown fond of Great Aunt Julia, she still had to smile at some of her ways.

'No wonder mine was so short!' she said. 'Why, she has written you pages and pages!'

'I felt quite overwhelmed when I saw it,' said Cyrus, with a curious mixture of groan and laugh. 'Say, I'm scared to meet an old lady who can pour words off her pen like that! Does she ever stop talking?'

'She doesn't waste words as a rule,' said Jill, 'but I suppose she thinks that her first letter to a long-lost cousin is not a thing to be scamped.'

'She sure has not scamped it,' said Cyrus. 'But, fire away, Jill. I *must* get to know what it is all about before you go out on the farm, for it will take me a week to write a suitable answer. I shall have to burn lots of midnight oil to do it in that time.'

Jill lost no more time, but began,

'Dear Cousin,

'Having heard my grandfather speak of a brother of his who migrated in his early youth to the United States of America, I have often wondered whether this branch of our Family' ('Capital letter, of course,' from Jill) 'had died out, or whether the heirs of the migrant Lomax were still extant.'

'What does it mean?' asked Cyrus feebly. 'I thought migrants were birds.'

'They are sometimes,' said Jill. 'She just means that she had thought there might be some Lomaxes in the States.'

'Ah! Well, what's next?'

'But for the magnitude of the task, and my own disinclination to cross the Atlantic and attend to the matter personally I should have pursued close investigations with the hope of tracing some of my kindred,' Jill went on.

'I am delighted to know that my great-great-uncle is now represented by one of his descendants, who is possessed of a right and fitting desire to cultivate the acquaintance of the English, and older branch of the Family.

'I should beg you to hasten to call on me, but I propose to visit the farm myself shortly, and as you tell me that your stay is so agreeable, I should be loath to shorten or even to interrupt it.

'As you have already passed through London, I expect you would prefer not to re-visit it so soon, and I shall therefore resign myself to deferring our meeting for a few days, when I shall be delighted to take the hand of another bearer of the name of which I am, I hope justly, proud.

'Believe me to be,

'Your kinswoman,

'JULIA LOMAX.'

'There's worse to come,' said Cyrus with a sigh. 'Look on the other side, Jill. She's drawn a sort of staircase gone crazy, with names stuck on the steps.'

Jill turned the page hastily, for she could not think what her cousin meant.

'It's a family tree,' she said. 'Like the

charts of the Kings of England. Ah, but you can't be expected to know about those, Cousin Cyrus, because your Presidents aren't descended from each other.'

'I guess not!' said Cyrus, feebly. 'But what have the Kings of England got to do with Great Aunt J.'s letter?'

'Nothing,' said Jill, who saw that her attempted explanation had only complicated matters. 'But they are set out in tables, just as Great Aunt Julia has set out the different members of the Lomax family. Here is the Lomax who went to America—your great-great-grandfather, and Aunt Julia's grandfather's brother.'

'Wait a bit,' said Cyrus, with his hand to his forehead. 'Great Aunt Julia's grandfather's brother. Oh, yes!'

'She couldn't fill in *his* descendants, you see,' Jill continued, 'but she has put a line for each generation till she came to you.'

'The other half is well filled in,' remarked Cyrus.

'Rather! Great Aunt Julia knows all about everybody. She can rattle off birthdays, maiden names of people who married into the family, how many children they all had, and lots more besides.'

'This will be Great Aunt J., I take it,' said Cyrus, pointing to the words. 'Julia Lomax, spinster.'

'Yes,' said Jill. 'Her brother was Dad's father, you see. Here's Dad, and a line to show that Emmeline, Freddie, Gwen and I are his children.'

'It gets pretty complicated if she fills in all your descendants by and by,' said Cyrus. 'There's no end to it! I look quite lonely all by myself on the other side of the staircase.'

'Don't let Great Aunt Julia hear you call it that!' warned Jill. 'She's got a proper family-tree drawn with all the names of Lomaxes for generations back on the branches.'

'And to think I'm a lone twig,' said Cyrus. 'My Dad was the only child, and his father's sisters—he had no brothers—all died unmar-

ried. I was the only member of the family
left when Dad died. I guess that's why I felt
I wanted to come and seek you out.'

'It must be horrid to feel you are all alone,'
said Jill softly. Cyrus had told them the day
before that his mother had died when he was
a baby, and that he had the haziest recol-
lection—more like a dream than a memory—
of her face.

'Now that I have found a family, I shan't
be in a hurry to leave it,' said Cyrus, his
usual cheerful smile banishing the sadness
with which he had spoken of being alone. 'I've
fixed things that I needn't go back for a good
spell, and I mean to enjoy my holiday over
here—if Great Aunt J. will let me,' he added
with another look at the formidable letter.

'She's jolly decent,' said Jill. 'The family
happens to be her pet subject. She was always
telling us when we were kids what was
expected of a Lomax! But you'll get on fine
with her, I feel sure. Even Gwen isn't afraid
of her now.'

'Then for very shame, I mustn't be afraid either,' laughed Cyrus, 'but do tell me how to write to her, Jill. I don't want to offend her in any way.'

'That won't do!' Jill declared stoutly. 'She'd know my style at once. I write to her regularly, you see. Just write what you think.'

'But you'll cast your eye over it, and tell me if I have put in anything that's likely to shock the old dame,' he begged.

'Oh, I'll do that, if you like,' said Jill. 'But I'm sure your letter will be quite all right. There's the clock striking! We mustn't be late for breakfast.'

Emmeline looked sharply at Jill as she and Cyrus entered the dining-room together.

'Where ever have you been, Jill?' she asked peevishly.

'In the little writing-room,' said Jill, in as offhand manner as she could assume. Something in her sister's tone sent the colour flaming to her cheeks.

Mr. Lomax came in just then, and Emmeline said no more. Jill hurried out after breakfast with the excuse that she wanted to see about some grain for the poultry. She kept out of the way till dinner-time, and after the others had left the room, Cyrus came back with a paper in his hand.

'I've just written a few lines to the lady,' he said. 'If you'll run your eye over them—— ?'

'Oh, yes,' said Jill, looking at the paper and avoiding his eye. The letter was short.

'Dear Cousin,

'I guess I can't figure out what relation you are, but I shall be real glad to meet you when you come to the farm, and if you'd like an escort should be pleased to run up to London and fetch you. I'm glad to find that my name gives me a passport to your favour, and hope to improve your acquaintance.

'Yours faithfully,
CYRUS J. LOMAX.'

'Will it do?' asked the writer anxiously. 'I've had some tough mails to deal with in my time, but I was never so put to it to write a letter.'

'It's a bit stiff,' said Jill, 'but it rings true, so I guess it will suit Great Aunt Julia.'

'Say now, don't you mock me with your "I guess"!'

'I didn't mean to mock you,' said Jill, with a blush, 'but you say it so often that I can't help using the expression too.'

'Well, I'll forgive you this time. I find myself using more Yankee slang over here than I did on the other side of the pond.'

'That's like Mr. Britling's American visitor,' said Jill, 'you think that we must be expecting you to speak with a strong American accent and use no end of slang, and so you do it to oblige us!'

'I guess that's it!' said Cyrus. 'Well, if you think I've got nothing in the letter that the old lady might think disrespectful, I'll post it right away.'

'You might take mine at the same time,' said Jill.

'Sure!' said Cyrus, 'but if you could spare time for a walk, we could go along to that little old post-office together.'

'I—I'm afraid I can't spare time,' said Jill, haltingly.

Cyrus felt disappointed and his face fell as Jill went out of the room.

'She's not going to do the shy coy maiden, I hope!' he said to himself. 'That frank way she had was just what made me take to her! I can't stick a mincing miss!'

To understand Jill's change of manner towards her cousin, we must go back to the look which Emmeline had given her at break-fast-time.

Emmeline had 'felt it her duty' as she said, to speak to Jill about her conduct. She had caught Jill when she went to wash before dinner, and said to her, 'Jill, I don't think you can realize how your behaviour strikes other people.'

'What's that?' said Jill, who had her face in the towel, and had not heard all that her sister said.

'You are not quite a child,' Emmeline went on severely, 'and you can't run round after a man without causing comment. You spend nearly all your time with Cousin Cyrus. That is the last way to win his respect.'

'Who on earth wants to "win his respect"?' asked Jill. 'You know that I never care a toss what people think!' Her cheeks burned as she spoke.

'You might spare *my* feelings! I get the blame for your hoydenish ways! And if you have set your cap at this fellow, let me advise you not to show it quite so plainly, or you will most likely defeat your own ends!'

Jill bit her lips, and did not speak until she had choked back the angry retort that occurred to her. When she had her feelings well under control, she said very quietly, 'I am not going to quarrel with you, Emmy, but you are making a big mistake.'

'I'm not a fool,' said Emmeline hotly. 'Do you think I can't see through your pretences?'

Jill did not answer. It was all she could do to go down to the dining-room and join in the conversation there as if nothing had happened. But the old frank relationship with Cyrus had been destroyed by her sister's unjust accusation.

CHAPTER VI

A FAMILY PARTY

Jill had to resort to many little subterfuges to avoid Cyrus without seeming to do so. After Emmeline's unkind remarks, she did not feel sufficiently at ease with him to seek his company, especially when no one else was present. Preparations for the holidays gave her an excuse to be too busy for reading or conversation, and at meal times she took care to chat away to every one in her old good-humoured way.

'Perhaps I was getting a bit too fond of hanging round to talk to him, instead of finding a job of work!' Jill said to herself. 'But Emmeline needn't have put that construction on it — I had no thought of running after him! He was a good pal, but I feel a fool when he speaks to me now. I wonder what made Emmeline flare out like that.'

Now Emmeline had been rather captivated by the visitor and had tried to monopolize his attention on the first evening. She had been so piqued at his showing far more interest in Jill than in herself, that the 'reproof' to Jill had been the result.

All things considered, Emmeline thought that this would be a good time to encourage the advances of a young farmer who had been paying her attentions which she had formerly been inclined to laugh at, and bashful Dicky Dodd became a regular visitor at the farm.

Jill liked Dicky, in a protecting, motherly sort of way, and she would have been very cordial to him but for the fear of incurring Emmeline's wrath. But she was glad when Dicky looked in for the evening, as she could often slip away to the little room over the porch, and snatch an hour for reading and dreaming.

The others were settled down to a game of cards on the evening before Gwen and Great Aunt Julia were expected and Jill thought it a fine chance to finish a book in which she was particularly interested.

'I shall get an hour to myself before supper', she thought, and when Betty came to the door to speak to her, she went out and did not return.

She was coiled up on the window-seat, making the most of the waning light, when she heard a firm footstep on the stairs. She knew whose it was, but before she had time to scramble off the seat and take a chair, her cousin entered the room.

'Say now, don't stir, Cousin Jill,' he said. 'I've come up to sit here too, but that is not going to drive you away!'

There was a masterful tone in his voice which Jill had never heard before.

'I thought you were playing cards,' she said.

'We were, but Mr. Lomax took my hand so that I could come up and write a letter.'

He did write a letter, but it was a very short one. When he had sealed it, he took a

book, and sat at the other end of the window-
seat.

'It's getting dark,' said Jill, 'I'll get a
lamp.'

'Not on my account, I hope,' was the reply.
'I'd just as soon sit here in the twilight, and
talk to you, Cousin Jill. You've been neglect-
ing me lately, you know.'

'Have I?' asked Jill.

'I've missed you, but I know you are
always busy. I guess I shall have to join the
staff, Jill. What job will you give me? I'm
game for anything!'

'Then you shall be Great Aunt Julia's
special bodyguard,' said Jill. 'You shall drive
to the station and meet her and Gwen to-
morrow.'

'I thought I heard you say you always met
the lady,' said Cyrus.

'Well, I've never had an American cousin
to send before,' said Jill. 'You'll go, won't
you?'

'Yes, if you come to support me,' said

Cyrus. 'I don't like to meet her by myself. If you are there you can kick me if I say anything that might offend her.'

'She's not so easily offended as you seem to think,' said Jill. 'I shall have to go, or Gwen will never forgive me. But if you'd rather meet Great Aunt Julia in the house, with the whole of the family to "support" you, there's no reason why you shouldn't.'

'I guess the old lady would think it more attentive of me to go along with you,' said Cyrus. 'That's settled then. I say, Jill, there's nothing the matter, is there? You seem a little quiet these days.'

'Oh, no!' said Jill, forcing a laugh, 'what should there be the matter?'

She put her book back on the shelf as she spoke and went towards the door.

'I'll ask Betty to bring you a light,' she said.

Cyrus did not answer, but he stayed in the little writing-room till supper-time. Jill joined the card players, and looked over her father's hand.

No one else volunteered to go to the station, so Jill and Cyrus set off together.

'You may have to walk back,' Jill warned him. 'I don't know how we could squeeze you and Great Aunt Julia into one of these seats.'

'I could sit on the floor,' said Cyrus.

Jill had forgotten all embarrassment over Cyrus's company in her delight at seeing Gwen again. Her eyes shone and there was a delighted flush on her brown cheeks.

'I should like to see her look like that if she were coming to meet me,' thought Cyrus.

Jill did a little jig on the platform as the train drew in. She was waving excitedly.

'There's Gwen! I knew she'd be at the window. Doesn't she look grown-up?' She forgot that Cyrus had never seen her before. 'Darling Gwen! I thought the term would never end!'

Gwen had tumbled out of the carriage by this time and was in Jill's arms. She had no eyes for her sister's companion, though she had heard that he would be at the farm for

the holidays, until Jill said, 'This is Cousin
Cyrus, Gwen.'

The greeting between them was short, for
Great Aunt Julia appeared in the carriage
doorway. Jill saw at a glance that the 'Family'
was even more to the fore than usual. Miss
Lomax had marked the occasion by wearing
a huge gold watch with a heavy bunch of
seals—a family heirloom which only saw the
light at rare intervals. Her manner had an
added stateliness which was all the more
apparent beside the affectionate greeting
between the sisters.

Jill, however, was quite undaunted.

'How are you, Great Aunt Julia?' she cried.
'It's fine to see you again. Cousin Cyrus is
here, you see. He couldn't wait at home to
meet you!'

She gave the old lady her right hand; the
left was clasping Gwen. Miss Lomax smiled
at her, and said. 'I am delighted to see you,
Jill. Cousin, this is a great pleasure to me!
I can see at once that you are a Lomax! To

think that I should have been unaware of your existence all these years!'

She gave him her hand, and Cyrus wrung it heartily. He had been looking shrewdly at the old lady, and there was something about her that he liked.

'I'm real glad to find another cousin,' he said. 'I'm having a dandy time at the farm. I guess it was the best day's work I ever did when I made up my mind to come to England for a spell.'

Jill had got the luggage by this time, and she and Gwen were carrying it to the trap. Cyrus was about to hurry after them to take it, but Great Aunt Julia signed to him to stay with her.

'Jill doesn't need a porter,' she said. 'Haven't you found that out yet? She would carry half a ton with one hand, so long as she could hold Gwen with the other.'

'She's a good sort,' said Cyrus.

'Ah, she is! But now tell me, what other relatives have you in America?'

'I'm the one and only Lomax on the other side, to the best of my belief!'

'To think of that!' said Great Aunt Julia. 'I must hear more about your ancestors when we get to the farm. I can tell you all there is to be known about the English branch.'

They had now reached the trap, and Cyrus politely handed Miss Lomax into the empty seat opposite the two girls.

'Where do you sit?' asked Great Aunt Julia abruptly.

'Cousin Jill warned me I might have to walk back,' Cyrus began.

'Stuff and nonsense. I don't take up so much room as all that. Come you here, Gwen; surely you can tear yourself away from Jill for half an hour. You will still be able to look at her, you know. Now, Cyrus, sit by Jill.'

It was a tight squeeze for them all, but no one seemed to mind. Great Aunt Julia was deep in pedigrees for the benefit of Cyrus, who was much more interested in the glowing young faces of Jill and Gwen. He maintained some appearance of interest for politeness' sake, but his attention wandered far more than Great Aunt Julia thought.

'Dear old Daddy!' cried Gwen, 'it's lovely to see you looking so strong again! How's Emmy? Hulloa, Freddie! Where's Betty?'

She ran from one to the other with Jill at her heels. Great Aunt Julia gave her usual stern greeting to Emmeline, looked hard at Freddie to see what fault she could find with him, and congratulated Mr. Lomax on his improved health.

Having thus discharged her obligations as a visitor and a relative, she turned her whole attention to Cyrus, who was soon so overwhelmed with a mass of information about Lomaxes and their history, that he found himself longing for Jill to come to the rescue.

She came at last, and brought tea with her, so Great Aunt Julia had to put up the documents she had brought, much to the relief of Cyrus, who was trying to think of some excuse to escape from the farm for the remainder of Miss Lomax's visit.

He confided his plan to Jill later in the evening.

'I guess I can't stick a fortnight of this,' he said feebly. 'It's enough to turn a fellow's brain! And you weren't there to support me, Jill! I was counting on you, you know!'

'I had such heaps to say to Gwen,' said Jill. 'I thought you got on splendidly with Great Aunt Julia at the station and on the way home.'

'She hadn't got her steam up then,' sighed Cyrus. 'I did rather take to her, but it's a pity that she can't talk about something else besides the family.'

'Oh, she will,' said Jill, 'she's the sort who likes to get things off her chest as quickly as possible. You fill up your family-tree for her, and as you finish, I'll try to give you an opening to talk about some of the things you were telling us last week. I'm sure she'd be

interested. You're a very good conversational-
ist, you know. While you are talking, she'll
have to listen!'

'I don't know about that!' said Cyrus, 'talk
about conversation! I can talk some, I know,
but she has got me beaten to a frazzle!'

He took Jill's advice, however, and took his
cue smartly when she gave it. For the rest of
the evening Cyrus was the talker. Family
affairs were dropped and they all listened to
accounts of his life in America and his travels
on both sides of the Atlantic.

When he flagged, Jill, ever watchful of
Great Aunt Julia, brought up some fresh topic
which started him off again. They were all
surprised to find that the evening had gone
so quickly, and Cyrus himself seemed amazed
at his success.

'You've got a head on you, Jill,' he whispered as he passed her in the hall after
supper. 'That did the trick, just as you said!'

'You kept us all interested,' said Jill. 'I've
never seen Great Aunt Julia so attentive to

anyone's conversation before. You'd better start giving lectures.'

'I should never have thought of it if you hadn't suggested it,' he said. 'Fancy my daring to speak for a couple of hours on end, with Great Aunt J. in the room! I shall look to you to back me again, Jill!'

'Your servant, sir,' said Jill merrily.

Great Aunt Julia unbent to Cyrus almost as much as she did to Jill; she asked him to take her for drives; she consulted him on business matters; she invited him to spend a long visit at her London home, and she showed him pretty plainly that she approved of him.

She praised him to Jill when she was alone with the girl, and was surprised to find her only mildly enthusiastic on the subject of the American cousin.

'I thought from the way you wrote about him when he first came that you and he were very good friends,' she said, giving Jill one of her sharpest glances.

'Oh, we're very good friends,' said Jill carelessly. 'But I don't go around raving about him, as Emmeline does about that Dicky Dodd.'

'You don't appear to me to have much to say to him,' said Great Aunt Julia. Jill remembered the little conspiracy on the night of her arrival, and smiled inwardly.

'I think you might be a little more cordial to a relative,' said Great Aunt Julia. 'It's not like you to be inhospitable.'

Still Jill did not reply.

'Come!' said the old lady impatiently. 'I want to know what you are thinking of!'

'Well,' said Jill reluctantly, 'if I must tell you, it is this — Emmy gave me a hint that I was being too friendly with him when he first came. All rot, of course, but it made me feel a little embarrassed when he was about.'

'Emmeline is a fool!' said Miss Lomax testily. 'And I shall think you are another, Jill, if you take the slightest notice of her nonsense!'

Jill laughed at her great aunt's vehemence.

'Don't tell her that I've said anything about it to you, will you? I'm not even telling Gwen.'

'Oh, I'll say nothing! But it's a thousand pities she can't mind her own business.'

'It's nothing, really,' Jill went on, 'but after she had spoken to me like that, I thought I wouldn't give her the chance to say any more.'

But thinking over the conversation later on, Jill was quite at a loss to understand why Great Aunt Julia had felt so strongly about the matter.

CHAPTER VII

A THUNDERBOLT

Jill and Gwen sat at their window talking long after the rest of the family had gone to sleep. At last Gwen began to yawn, and Jill said, 'There! I've kept you up much too late. Draw the curtains while I light the candle.'

'Jill,' said Gwen softly, as she rose to do as her sister suggested, 'do look! There are two men skulking under the hedge on the other side of the lane.'

Jill paused with a match in one hand and the box in the other, and peered out into the moonlight.

'They are in the shadow,' she said, 'but I can just make them out. What can they be doing there?'

'Do you think they are burglars?' asked Gwen nervously.

'Burglars wouldn't show themselves as early as this,' said Jill decidedly. 'It's nothing to worry about, Gwen. Watch will bark himself hoarse if they so much as touch the gate or wall. I wonder he hasn't started already, for he just hates prowlers.'

'Perhaps they've poisoned him,' said Gwen, holding tightly to Jill's arm.

'No, no!' replied Jill, 'I can see him walking about the yard. But look, Gwen! One of the men is pointing up at our windows. Can he see us, do you think?'

'Not in these navy dresses,' said Gwen, after a pause. 'The room must be much darker than the road. They wouldn't be able to see into it. Are you lighting the candle now, Jill?'

'No, ducky, we'll go to bed without it, for once. You know just where everything is, don't you?'

'Of course,' said Gwen, 'but, Jill, what is happening?'

'Nothing of any consequence, no doubt,' said Jill, 'I just thought we needn't draw the attention of those men to the fact that there is any one awake here. Let them think no one has seen them.'

'I shall be too nervous to go to sleep,' declared Gwen.

'Why, you little goose!' said Jill. 'Who's going to hurt you! I'd take care of you, whatever happened.'

'Oh, yes, Jill, I'm sure you would!'

'There's nothing here for burglars to steal,' said Jill. 'I don't think they would waste their time on us, with so many big houses close by. Go to sleep at once, goosey!'

Gwen protested that this was impossible, but as Jill refused to talk once they were in bed, she soon did fall asleep. Jill waited until her regular breathing showed that she was not likely to be easily roused, and then slipped softly out of bed. She wanted to see if the men were still there. She could see nothing, but she thought she heard a sound from the room across the landing, where Cousin Cyrus slept.

Jill's heart began to thump very uncomfortably. She had previously been pleased to think how calm she had kept.

'It might be as well to warn him,' she thought. 'He has a lot of money with him, and it may have got talked about. He is rather careless with his rolls of notes when he goes shopping. People must have seen him, and gossip goes the round so quickly in a little country place.'

By this time she had got into slippers and dressing-gown, and was carefully opening her door.

'There's no need to rouse the house,' she thought. 'If there is anything up, Cyrus will be the best one to help me deal with it.'

A light shone in at the landing window for a moment as she spoke. Then it vanished, leaving Jill's eyes dazzled for a few minutes.

'That might have been some sort of signal,' she said. 'I won't lose any time.'

She tapped softly at the door, but got no answer.

'Perhaps he went to the writing-room,' she said. 'He has bad nights sometimes, I think, and sits up to read until he is sleepy.'

She remembered that Cyrus had said something about reading at night when he first came to the farm.

But the little room over the porch was quite empty, and everything was just as she had left it earlier in the evening. No books were missing from the familiar rows on the shelves. The volume she had put on the table lay just where she had left it. She went back to the bedroom door and tapped again, a little louder this time.

The door was not latched, and it swung open at her touch. The moonlight now flooded the room, and Jill saw at a glance that it was empty, and that the bed had not been touched.

'Where can he be?' thought Jill. 'Did he, too, see those men, and go down alone to grapple with them? I can't go back to bed without knowing more of this strange business.'

She groped her way downstairs and went into every room. Nothing had been disturbed as far as she could tell. The doors were all secured as usual. But there was no trace of Cyrus.

'Perhaps he got fed up with sleeping alone and went to share Freddie's room,' said Jill, when she had made perfectly certain that he was not on the ground floor. 'I can hardly barge in to make sure, but I hate mysteries, and could wish that people didn't change their rooms without warning. It might lead to all sorts of complications.'

She sometimes ran in with a cold sponge and presented it to Freddie when he was loath to rise.

'I mustn't prowl about any longer, or I shall be waking some one,' she said, as she went softly upstairs.

Gwen had not stirred, and Jill crept into bed beside her, so tired after her long day that even the mysteries of the night could not keep her awake.

She was up even earlier than usual the next morning, for she had made up her mind to do as much as she could before breakfast, so as to have more spare time to spend with Gwen.

Gwen, free from the tyranny of a rising bell still slept on, and Jill was careful not to rouse her. She was the first up; even old Betty was not yet stirring, and she opened the kitchen door to get the first breath of spring air.

It was too early for the milking, but she got her pails together, and then went back to the house and began to do little tasks that would lighten Betty's labour during the day. As soon as the cowman came, she started milking, and sang contentedly to herself as she worked.

'Gwen didn't say what she thought of him last night,' Jill said to herself, in an interval between two songs, 'but I am sure she likes him. And he likes her; I could tell that by the way he looked at her. But she's not such a baby as he seemed to think, after all.'

It occurred to her to ask the cowman if he

had seen any strangers hanging about the night before. Jill felt sure that none of the villagers would be watching the farm so late at night.

'I seed two outcomers at the station when I went wi' the milk. From London, I should say they were, Miss Jill. Come to think on it, they axed about you and the 'Merican and the old lady.'

'What did they want to know?' asked Jill.

'What were yer names, and where the 'Merican come from and that,' said the man. 'I never told 'em much, for I didn't like the way they had wi' 'em. Too smart by half, I thought they were.'

'Well, any one might have asked that just from curiosity,' said Jill. 'You didn't see them again, I suppose.'

'No, but I hear there were two strangers at the Cross Keys last night, very friendly and talkative they were, too, Joe Williams said. I suppose 'twere the same 'uns, but I couldn't be sure.'

Jill thought no more of the two strangers, for Gwen came running out to reproach her for letting her sleep on when she might have been helping.

'You come at a good time with your offers of help,' said Jill. 'I've just finished, as you see. But it must be nearly breakfast-time. Are the others about?'

'I met Dad in the yard with Freddie as I came out,' said Gwen. 'I haven't seen any one else.'

They found Emmeline in the dining-room waiting for them, and Great Aunt Julia was not long after. Then Freddie and Mr. Lomax came in, and looked round for Cyrus.

'Where's Cousin Cyrus?' said Mr. Lomax. 'This is the first time I have known him late for breakfast.'

Jill felt vaguely uneasy without quite knowing why.

'I'll run up and call the lazy bounder,' said Freddie with a grin. 'Jill, where's that big sponge you so kindly bring for me?'

'I don't expect you will need it,' said Jill. 'Very likely he is writing letters or reading in the little room over the porch. I don't think he ever oversleeps.'

'He may have strolled out and gone farther than he intended,' put in Great Aunt Julia. 'He was telling me how much he enjoyed the fresh bright mornings here.'

Freddie's step was heard coming hastily downstairs. Something made them all turn to the door as he entered.

'What's the matter, Freddie?' cried Jill.

'He's not there!'

'Not there?'

'Not in his room—not in the house anywhere. His bed hasn't been slept in!'

'What's the matter?' asked Betty, who came in with eggs just as Freddie finished speaking.

'Cousin Cyrus has disappeared,' said Emmeline.

'You don't say so,' said the old woman. 'Well, to be sure! And where can the poor lad be got to? I call to mind now ye speak of him that I haven't seen him about this morning, and he's generally in the way to give me a hand with the pails and what not.'

'Jill,' said Gwen, 'do you think that those two men we saw hanging about in the lane last night had anything to do with Cousin Cyrus's disappearance?'

'I don't know,' said Jill. 'How should I? But I wish you wouldn't all keep talking about his disappearance so glibly. Wasn't Great Aunt Julia saying only a few minutes ago that he might have walked farther than he intended to?'

Mr. Lomax rose from the table. 'Excuse me, Aunt, and you too, girls. I will go up with Freddie and see if I can get to the bottom of this business. Don't spoil your breakfast on account of it, I beg.'

Emmeline poured out the coffee, and the girls and their aunt made some show of starting their breakfast, but they were all listening intently to the footsteps overhead.

Mr. Lomax looked very puzzled when he came back.

'He evidently meant to go,' he said. 'He has packed his bag hastily, as far as we could gather, so presumably he went of his own accord. But why he should treat us in so summary a way, I am completely at a loss to understand.'

Jill sat speechless with astonishment and dismay. What could this mean? Why should Cyrus go off without saying a word to any one? And did he know anything about those men who had been outside the farm the night before?

'Gwen said something about two men,' said Emmeline. 'Where did you see them, Gwen, and when?'

'They were under the hedge on the other side of the lane when Jill and I went to bed last night,' said Gwen, 'we saw them about twelve o'clock. We sat talking without a light for a long time after we went upstairs and when we found they were there, Jill said we wouldn't attract their attention by lighting a candle.'

'Why didn't you tell me all this, Jill?' asked her father.

'Well, I didn't see you till I came in to breakfast, Dad,' said Jill, 'and as everything was quite all right when I got downstairs, I didn't think it was of any importance.'

'It's a wonder that we weren't all murdered in our beds,' said Emmeline, affecting to shudder.

'Watch would have barked if they had come to the gate,' said Jill quietly.

'I'm not so sure,' said Emmeline scornfully. 'You know your Cousin Cyrus made a point of being friendly with that dog. He was always petting him. No doubt his accomplices knew that he had got round the dog.'

'His *what*?' cried Jill hotly.

'You needn't flare up!' said Emmeline. 'It's pretty clear to me that those wretches were in league with him and that they went off together on some nefarious scheme.'

'You are assuming a little too much, Emmy,' said Mr. Lomax quietly, after a distressed look at Jill's flushed cheeks.

'Well, it looks precious fishy,' said Freddie.

'Of course it does,' said Emmeline. 'Even Jill would see that if she wasn't so infatuated with the man.'

'Come, come,' said Great Aunt Julia sharply. 'There is no need to malign a man because he chooses to slip away without saying "Good-bye". *I* may have scared him off, for all I can tell you! He has shown himself sadly lacking in politeness, it is true, but for the present we will leave it at that, if you please.'

Emmeline could scarcely pursue the topic after this rebuke and the subject was dropped. Those who felt inclined to eat finished their breakfast, but Jill could only make the merest pretence of eating. She was thankful that the cat had crept into the room, and he benefited by her lack of appetite. With this willing aid, she cleared her plate, and she was heartily thankful when the others left the table.

Before she started work, she found a chance of speaking to Great Aunt Julia.

'You don't think that Cousin Cyrus is — is?'

She was at a loss to finish the sentence.

'I reserve judgement,' said the old lady. 'I did not expect this, I can tell you, and I am generally a good judge of character. But Jill, there is no need for you to worry so much, whatever he has done. There is no reflection on any of us. He may not even be a Lomax. Any imposter might have known that a member of our family went to America, and might have been prepared to use that knowledge to get shelter here for a time. That he resembles the family may be coincidence.'

'That's possible,' said Jill, 'for indeed, we know no more of him than what he chose to tell us. But, somehow, I can't think of him as a scoundrel.'

She turned away without saying any more.

'I won't speak to any one about him again,'

she determined, 'not even to Gwen. They will get suspicious if I say too much about him, or take his part. Oh dear, I wish he had never come! It seemed so jolly to have him at first, but now——!'

CHAPTER VIII

WANTED!

Gwen was entertaining the family with college news and jokes that evening, when Betty put her head in at the door to announce a visitor.

'Some one to see the master,' she said briefly; then she withdrew and left the caller to enter the room without further ceremony.

They had not been expecting a visitor, for it was getting late. Dicky Dodd was in his usual place at Emmeline's side, trying hard to look as if he were not afraid of Great Aunt Julia. Gwen and Jill sat on a low seat by the fire, and Miss Lomax and her nephew sat on opposite sides of the hearth. Freddie strolled about the room, or stood with his elbow on the end of the mantelpiece as he felt disposed.

Every one missed Cyrus, even Gwen and

Miss Lomax, who had seen so little of him, but they all avoided any reference to him, however remote.

'Pray don't let me disturb you,' said a quiet voice. 'I shall be quite distressed if the ladies spoil that charming group. If you will come with me to another room, Mr. Lomax, we can soon dispose of the little business which unfortunately interrupts you at such an unseasonable time.'

'He doesn't mean the business to be put off,' thought Jill, noticing the firm tone in which the caller spoke. 'I wonder who he is — surely he is not come on farm affairs at this time in the evening.'

With an apologetic glance at Miss Lomax and the girls, Mr. Lomax took the visitor to his little office. He did not close the door behind them, but the caller took the liberty of doing so.

'I don't think I have had the pleasure of meeting you before,' Mr. Lomax began.

'No,' replied the other. 'But I will state

my business as briefly as possible. I want to see your visitor.'

'You are rather peremptory!' said Mr. Lomax, not too well pleased at the abrupt announcement. 'And you need not have troubled to come here, if that is all you want. She is in the dining-room with the others. Surely you saw her!'

'Perhaps I ought to warn you that I am a police-officer and that to obstruct me in the carrying out of my duties is a serious offence.'

Mr. Lomax looked very surprised.

'I shall do all I can to assist you, officer,' he answered, 'but I am completely at a loss to know what you can want with so obviously respectable a lady as Miss Lomax.'

'You are making a mistake,' said the officer. 'It's no woman that I'm after. As you persist in taking this line, which doesn't deceive me in the least, I must search the premises.'

'At least you will not object to showing me your authority——'

'Of course you are entitled to see it!' broke

in the other. 'Here is a warrant for the arrest of Hyram D. Seddons, otherwise known as "Flash Jack". He is wanted on a number of charges and we have had some trouble in tracing him down to this part, I can tell you.'

Mr. Lomax put his hand to his head. 'I have never heard of him!' he declared.

'Now, sir, for your own sake, you had better be frank with me. There's such an offence as "aiding and abetting", you know. If you think to help this fellow, you are making a mistake, and putting yourself in a very awkward position at the same time.'

'If you won't believe me,' said Mr. Lomax, 'perhaps you will believe the rest of my family. You are at liberty to question them, either singly or together, before me, or in my absence. I cannot say fairer than that.'

He led the way back to the dining-room as he spoke.

'This gentleman has something to ask you,' he said. 'This, sir, is my aunt, Miss Lomax, who came from London yesterday afternoon

with my youngest daughter' (he pointed to
Gwen) 'for a visit. My other daughters and
my son live at home. Mr. Dodd is a neighbour
who is spending the evening with us.'

Mr. Lomax retired to the window when he
had made this explanation, and left the caller
to proceed as he wished.

The little group round the fire was startled
at this strange introduction, especially as Mr.
Lomax showed no small annoyance and was
clearly exercising a good deal of self-restraint.
Jill's heart began to thump, for she thought
she knew what was coming. But even she was
not prepared for the officer's words.

'I want to know where your visitor—the
gentleman who has been staying here for
some time, not this lady' (with a bow to
Great Aunt Julia) 'is to be found.'

Emmeline broke the awkward silence.
'That is exactly what we cannot tell you,' she
said.

'I must know,' was the reply. 'I am a police-
officer with due authority to arrest him, and

I must warn you not to interfere with me in the execution of my duty.'

He brought out the official phrase with the fluency which came from constant use, and thought, 'Such an obstinate lot I never did see! Yet to look at 'em you would think it would all be plain sailing.'

A little gasp ran round the room.

Great Aunt Julia bridled and shook her head indignantly, as if to say, 'How *dare* you arrest a Lomax!'

Freddie gave a low whistle. Emmeline looked as if she could believe anything of the American, and had suspected him all along. Gwen looked scared, and Dicky Dodd wished, and showed very plainly that he wished, that he had chosen some other time for his visit.

But it was Jill who spoke. Her strained, unnatural voice fell strangely on the ears of the rest.

'I think there must be some mistake,' she said, firmly. 'Our only visitor, except the ones you see here, was a cousin, Cyrus J. Lomax, from New York.'

'He may be calling himself Abraham Lincoln or George Washington, Miss, for all I know! But I'm sure I'm not mistaken in my man. Where is he now? I can't have my time wasted like this, you know!'

'He left this morning,' said Jill.

The officer swallowed hard and looked at her suspiciously. 'Go on, Miss,' he said grimly, 'I must know all about it.'

'I'm afraid I can't tell you any more,' she said.

'But you must, Miss—I want to know everything you can tell me! Come, now!'

'We don't know any more,' said Mr. Lomax, coming to Jill's rescue. 'We are as much in the dark as you are. This man came to us a few weeks ago, saying he was a Lomax, the descendant of a member of the family who went to America many years ago. He was certainly not unlike the Lomaxes, and we had no reason to doubt his word. He stayed with us at our invitation but disappeared last night. His bed was not slept in, and we know of no reason why he should leave in this mysterious way. We parted at bedtime last night on our usual cordial terms. That is all I can tell you.'

The officer's face fell. 'I must search the house,' he said.

'I doubt if your warrant authorizes you to do that, but you have my full and free permission to go all over it,' said Mr. Lomax.

'Ah,' said the man. 'That's very good of you. I'll go at once if I may, then. I've wasted too much time already.'

Mr. Lomax took a candle from the hall table, and showed the visitor over the ground floor. He waited patiently while the officer examined each room, and when he had finished there, he took him upstairs.

'This was his bedroom,' said Mr. Lomax, 'it is left just as it was when I came up to look for him this morning. Nothing has been interfered with. These clothes and brushes and so on, belong to Mr. Lomax.'

The detective picked them up. 'Pretty complete,' he said, 'he's got the initials he was using on some of them, I see.'

'My servant will be able to tell you that his linen was marked with his full name. I remember that she remarked on it, not being used to washing clothes that were marked in this way. He has received a number of letters addressed in the same way—oh, you have found an envelope, I see.'

The man put it in his pocket stolidly, without making any comment, and the contents of a small wastepaper basket next came in for his scrutiny.

They went on to the other rooms. 'He did not enter any of the other rooms on this floor except the little writing-room, where my girls sometimes sit to read or write,' said Mr. Lomax, 'but as I said, you are at liberty to see the house from attic to cellar.'

The man went doggedly on with his search. He seemed to think that he was dealing with people so deep that he was bound not to omit the slightest precaution. He was so used to meeting with duplicity, and had come so sure of finding the wanted man, that he thought Mr. Lomax was shielding the criminal. But he did not quite know whether the willingness to show him every part of the house arose from a desire to gain time and so give the wanted man a good start, or whether it was a feint to put him off.

Great Aunt Julia had listened to every word and watched every look that passed while the detective was in the dining-room, but so far she had not spoken. By the time he returned from his search, however, she seemed to have made up her mind about the whole matter, and she was the first to speak when the two men came back.

'Are you satisfied?' she said shortly.

'I beg your pardon, ma'am?'

'Are you satisfied?' repeated the old lady sternly.

'I am satisfied that I needn't trespass on your time any more—at present—I mean,' was the reply. 'Allow me to wish you good night.'

He went out with a mysterious air which seemed to imply that he had not yet finished with them—that they might expect to see more of him before he *was* satisfied. Mr. Lomax showed him out, and came back with a puzzled look.

'A most amazing situation!' he said.

'Not at all!' said Emmeline. 'What did you expect of that fellow? He must have had some deep motive for skulking about here all that time! I never trusted him! But it is too bad of him to implicate us. It's a perfect disgrace.'

'I can't see that we are implicated, as you call it,' said Mr. Lomax. 'We have nothing to fear; we have been perfectly frank with the detective, as he will no doubt discover in good time.'

'He didn't seem to think so!' observed Freddie.

'Well, my boy, when a man spends his life

looking for criminals, he may be pardoned for
not recognizing straight dealing when he does
meet it! It's his business to suspect every one,
you know, and he seemed so sure in the first
place that the man he wanted was here, that
he was naturally incredulous, I may say
disappointed as well, when he found that he
was gone.'

'It's a pity Cousin Cyrus wasn't here so
that he could have seen his mistake for
himself,' said Gwen, speaking for the first
time since the caller had been announced.

'A great pity!' said Emmeline with a scorn-
ful laugh.

'I'm sure it was a mistake,' Gwen went on.
'I expect the man that he wanted was one of
those that we saw at the gate last night.'

'Perhaps it is just as well that you didn't
tell him that,' said Emmeline. 'He would only
have taken it for another cock-and-bull story
to put him off the scent. I think it was a great
mistake to attempt to shield the man in any
way.'

'I am not aware that any one did try to shield him,' said Great Aunt Julia. 'You are a little too sure of yourself, Emmeline. Let me tell you that, criminal or no criminal, the man who sat in that chair last night is a Lomax—I would take my oath on that. As to my opinion about his honesty, I will say nothing at present. Time will tell!'

Jill's face cleared a little at this announcement.

'I think we ought to have told the man about those two men that the girls saw, don't you, Father?' said Freddie. 'They weren't up to any good, I am sure. It's his job to look out for suspicious characters. We don't want ricks burnt, or anything of that sort.'

'You are right, Freddie,' said Mr. Lomax, 'it would have been as well to mention it, and if I see the detective again, I will make a point of telling him. It is for him to decide whether the clue is worth following up.'

Jill slipped out of the room and went for her coat. No one guessed what was in her mind, for it was nearly supper-time, and she often went out to the kitchen about that time in the evening.

'I will run after that detective,' Jill resolved. 'He can't be gone very far. If I stand on the top bar of the gate I shall be able to see which way he went.'

It was a bright, clear night, and the moon was nearly full. Jill hurried out into the yard, anxious not to lose a moment.

She climbed to the top of the gate, but could see nothing. The lane was quite deserted. 'He has been very quick,' she said to herself. 'I shouldn't have thought it possible for him to get out of sight so soon. I'll go to the attic; the window gives a clear view of the lane in both directions, for quite a long way. I shall see round the curve of the lane there.'

She ran into the house, and mounted the stairs to the attic. She had not been mistaken, for the lane was empty.

'He had no car or horse waiting for him,' mused Jill. 'He can't have disappeared! Oh,

She climbed to the top of the gate, but could see nothing

I've got it! Of course! Just what the suspicious old thing would do!'

She went to her bedroom, and changed into Gwen's rubber gym shoes. She put on a dark coat, and pulled up the collar to hide her face as much as possible. Chuckling softly, she went downstairs again, and left the house by the back door. Watch was having his supper in the kitchen, and Betty was in the larder. No one had seen her manoeuvres so far. Keeping in the shadow of the house, she made her way to the bushes under the dining-room window. It was the only spot she meant to visit, as she knew it for the one place where the person she sought could hide on such a night.

She crept forward, parted the bushes, sprang on to a crouching figure which she saw there, and seized it by the arms, crying loudly, 'Help! Help!'

CHAPTER IX

JILL'S CAPTIVE

Mr. Lomax threw open the dining-room window — a French window, luckily — and sprang out as soon as he heard Jill's cry. Freddie was close after him, and he in turn was followed by Dicky Dodd.

Great Aunt Julia and the two girls came to the window to see what was going on. They could hear a terrific scuffle outside, but did not see much because the men's figures interposed between them and the bushes.

'What is it, Jill?' cried her father, who had recognized the girl's voice.

Jill's answer was muffled, but they managed to make out, 'A skulking fellow, Dad, under the bushes. Quick, I can't hold him much longer.'

Gwen darted to the lamp, and brought it to the window to throw a light on the little group outside. As soon as Freddie could make out the two figures rolling about among the bushes, he grabbed the nearest arm, which fortunately was not Jill's, and cried, 'All right, Jill! I've got him.'

Dicky Dodd sped forward to help, and as Jill freed herself, he took the other arm of the captive, whose incoherence made no impression on his detainers.

'Good for you, Jill!' cried Freddie, as they marched the man into the house. 'Where shall we put him, Father, while I race for the police?'

'Wait a bit!' said Mr. Lomax. 'We will hear what he has to say first. He may not have meant any harm.'

'Then he shouldn't prowl about under people's windows at this time of night,' said Freddie, who seemed delighted with the whole incident. 'Jill ought to have a medal.'

'How did you come to find him, Jill?' asked Great Aunt Julia, giving Jill one of her shrewd glances.

'I saw a form moving in the bushes, by the

window,' said Jill. 'My head was full of those men we had just been talking about—the two that Gwen and I saw, you know, and I thought we might get to know a little more about them if I collared this one.'

'I can't think how you got him,' said Dicky, admiringly, 'he's a hefty chap.'

'I sprang on him by surprise and bowled him over,' said Jill. 'He wasn't expecting to have any one come upon him like that, and I called for help as soon as I had got him. I could not have held him for long,' she added modestly.

The captive, who had devoted the interval to scraping mud out of his mouth, and settling his disordered clothing, now turned as if to go away, but the two men tightened their grip.

'No, you don't!' cried Freddie. 'Oh, my hat!' he added, as the man turned towards the light and he saw his face, 'Jill! You've caught the detective!'

'What!' cried Jill, with well-feigned amazement. 'Isn't it one of those men we saw last night? He's just the build of the taller one.'

Mr. Lomax approached to verify his son's statement.

'Dear me! Yes,' he said, with the merest suspicion of a twinkle in his eye. 'It *is* the detective. How unfortunate! You will allow me to apologize, I hope, Officer, for my daughter's unfortunate mistake!'

'Most unfortunate!' Great Aunt Julia chimed in.

'Of course my daughter thought you were there for some unlawful purpose,' Mr. Lomax went on, for the man did not speak, but stood looking from one to another in a sheepish manner. 'However, I cannot altogether regret that you have returned, even under such awkward circumstances, for my girls have something to tell you.'

'I expect he heard all about it while he was outside the window,' said Miss Lomax.

The detective cleared his throat. 'I'll take a note of the full circumstances, if the ladies will oblige with them,' he said stolidly, taking out his note-book. He offered no protest about his capture, though Freddie's handling had been far from gentle.

Jill told him the facts briefly, and the detective noted them in his book. He offered no comment on the information.

'Do you think that they had anything to do with Mr. Cyrus Lomax's disappearance?' asked Great Aunt Julia.

'Can't say, I'm sure, ma'am. Is there anything more I can do for you?'

'I don't think so, thank you,' said Mr. Lomax.

He showed the visitor out, taking him to the gate this time and waiting until he disappeared round the corner of the lane. When he got back to the dining-room, Jill was being teased about her 'catch'.

'I think Jill has the laugh of us,' said Mr. Lomax. 'She knew that she was catching the detective well enough, didn't you, Jill?'

Jill nodded. 'I went out to look for him, to call him back and let him know about those two men. He was out of sight, and I knew he could not have walked off so quickly. When I saw him in the bushes, I was awfully mad. Seeing how he was with Dad, I thought he could do with a lesson.'

'And you gave your lesson very well, Jill,' said Great Aunt Julia approvingly. 'The idea of his eavesdropping under the window. We had already told him all we had to tell.'

'Perhaps we had better keep it dark that Jill attacked a detective,' said Mr. Lomax, 'but I don't think we shall hear any more about the matter.'

Mr. Lomax was right. They heard no more of the detective. No one in the village saw him after that evening, so he evidently decided that he could do no good by remaining in the neighbourhood.

Freddie kept a watch for several nights, in case the two prowlers appeared again, but there was no sign of them, and the whole incident would have been speedily forgotten but for Cousin Cyrus's share in it.

Jill watched the papers anxiously to see if any arrest had been made, but no Hyram Seddons figured in them. She hoped as time went on that Cyrus himself would write to explain his hasty and unceremonious departure, or even that he would come back.

But days and weeks passed, and there was no news of him. Jill could not wholly hide her anxiety, and even Gwen's company did little to cheer her up. The presence of her sister and Miss Lomax meant that she had to be careful to show as little of her feelings as possible, for she often felt their anxious eyes on her, and she was afraid that they would find out the real reason for her depression.

And she was angry with herself, too, that she could not forget the man who had come into her life so strangely, and left it so abruptly. But even as she tried to forget, she knew that she was attempting the impossible. Jill's affectionate heart did not so easily cast off a friend.

CHAPTER X

A CHANGE

'Frederick,' said Miss Lomax one evening as she sat alone with her nephew. 'I think Jill needs a change. She had a good deal of anxiety and responsibility while you were ill, and although she bore it well at the time, I think it is telling on her now. Let her come back to London with me for a time.'

Miss Lomax had a shrewd idea that Jill had been badly hit by the trouble about Cyrus, but she was too thoughtful to speak of what the girl was bravely trying to hide, so she did not refer to that side of the question.

'Perhaps you are right, Aunt,' said Mr. Lomax. 'We are all so willing to rely on Jill that we don't always realize how much she does for us. By all means take her back with you. I shall miss her greatly, but the child deserves a holiday. I am well settled into work now, and have got my old grip—and more than my old grip—on my affairs. I must learn to do without her!'

'Learn to do without whom?' asked Jill, coming in as he finished speaking.

'Without you, my dear!' said Mr. Lomax. 'Great Aunt Julia wants to take you back to London for a holiday. She thinks you need a change.'

'I could be spared now almost better than at any other time of the year,' said Jill thoughtfully, 'and I could come back in good time for the haymaking. If you are sure that you can spare me, Dad, and will promise to write for me if you should want me specially, I should like to go back with Great Aunt Julia and Gwen.'

Mr. Lomax, who had expected a protest, was surprised at her acquiescence. 'Very good, my dear,' he said, 'I can undertake to promise that, I am sure. I will let you know just how I get on.'

'And if you find that the young woman is *not* indispensable, after all,' struck in Miss Lomax, 'we might go back to the old plan of making her a nurse.'

'Why,' said Jill, 'I put that idea aside long ago!'

'But there is no need for you to put it aside!' retorted Great Aunt Julia. 'It's time you learnt that folk *could* get on without you, my dear. I want to see what you will be like after you have been turned out in the world for a year or two.'

'I know I've a lot of corners to be rubbed off!' said Jill, smiling. 'But we must see how Dad gets on before we make any plans for my leaving home for good.'

'Quite so! Quite so!' said Miss Lomax, 'but I wanted you to keep the idea in your mind, Jill. At any rate you shall come to me for a month or two. That will give us all time to consider the matter fully.'

Jill went off to tell Gwen the news, and Miss Lomax said to her nephew, 'You can trust her to me, can't you, Frederick? I am as anxious for her happiness as you yourself.'

'I know it! I know it!' he replied. 'And I have been thinking ever since I began to get about a bit, that it is not fair to keep the girl at home. Emmeline will be getting married in a year or so, I gather, and it will be an excellent chance for her to get a little practice in being the mistress of a farmhouse.'

'You realize that Jill has been mistress, I see!' said Miss Lomax. 'Well, Mr. Dicky Dodd will be lucky if Emmeline learns to do what Jill has done this past couple of years! But I've hope for her—and Dicky—yet!'

Emmeline certainly was showing more interest in household matters, and she was learning to treat Betty with a little more tact. Mr. Dodd was happy to find his affection returned, and the two had made up their minds to marry and take over Dick's father's farm when the old gentleman retired.

'I shall miss you, Jill,' said Emmeline, when she heard that Jill was to go to London.

'I wish you would let me come around with you for the rest of the time you are at home, and see just how you do things. I shall never be able to keep the peace with old Betty unless I get into your ways.'

Jill was quite ready to do all she could to help her sister, and glad to think that Emmeline wanted to take her place. In the few days that remained of the holidays, the two sisters came nearer to understanding each other than they had ever done before.

Freddie was not at all pleased with the arrangement, but he knew it was no good objecting, so he confined his remarks to envious expressions about Jill's good luck. Betty frankly said that it was time the others did some of the work, instead of standing about looking on while Jill did it, and she was glad that Miss Lomax was going to make a lady of Jill.

'Make a lady of me!' cried Jill with a laugh. 'Why, Betty, I'm the last person to make what you call a lady! If Dad finds that he can spare me for good, I am going to be a nurse.'

'Don't you bother your head wi' looking
after strange folk!' counselled Betty. 'Get a
husband and family, Julie, and you'll have
enough to do without looking for strangers to
mind. I should like to take your little ones on
my lap before my old eyes get too dim to look
into their pretty faces.'

Jill's eyes were very bright as she answered
gaily, 'But, Betty, you are always saying what
a bother the men are, and how you could
never abide to have them about you!'

'Me and you, Julie, are two different people.
But there, you always were one to go your
own way, so I don't suppose anything old
Betty can say will make you alter your mind.'

'You'll send me a message when Emmeline
writes,' said Jill. 'I shall want to know just
how you are getting on.'

'I might make shift to write a line myself,
if so be as you wouldn't be too particular
about the spelling,' said old Betty, much to
Jill's delight.

'The spelling doesn't matter a bit!' declared

Jill. 'I shan't think about that, for I get in a muddle with the long words myself sometimes. And I'll answer every one the same day I get it, Betty, and tell you about the sights I see in London.'

'Ye mustn't expect me to be writing every two-three days, Julie,' said Betty, 'but I'll drop you a line when there's anything special to say—when the calves are sold, or the butter's extra good. I might be able to send ye butter for your own eating, Julie, for I don't hold no opinion whatever of that London stuff. There's folk in London, I'm sure on it, as don't know the taste of *butter*, not what I mean by butter, anyways.'

There was one little discovery Jill made when she packed her books which recalled memories that she had tried to push into the background. In an envelope on which her name was scrawled in a well-remembered hand, she found the roll of notes that she had given back to Cyrus. She knew they could not have been there on the last evening he spent at the farm, for she had been moving the books then to get one for Gwen.

'So he must have tossed them there for me to find when he went out of the house,' said Jill to herself, as she locked them safely away in her writing-case.

She half wanted to tell the others, if only to show that Cyrus had no ill-intentions as far as they were concerned, but somehow she could not speak of it, and so she kept the secret to herself.

CHAPTER XI

CORRESPONDENCE

My dearest Gwen,

I promised faithfully to let you know my first impressions of the hospital, so here goes. I felt very small and insignificant when I passed the porter at the gate last night, but I just managed to find enough voice to tell him that I was a new nurse, and he told me where to find the nurses' quarters in such a fatherly way that I am sure he must have known I had 'just come up'.

I reported to the Matron's office, but that was a mere form; the Matron was not there and the Assistant Matron who checked me in (I felt like a parcel being signed for) is quite human. I can't quite think of the Matron as an ordinary mortal yet, but I calm myself by recalling that she too, strange as it appears, was once a little pro. and liable to be blamed for anything and everything that went wrong in her ward!

My little bedroom is not bad; small of course, but as I have got it all to myself, I don't mind that. Here followeth the inventory of its contents:

One bed, comfy enough, but not by any means ornate — like the ones the patients sleep in, in fact.

One wardrobe with sizeable drawer at bottom; will hold all the clothes I bothered to bring without any overcrowding.

One dressing chest, one bedroom chair, one easy ditto. The last is a recent luxury and the nurses haven't got over their surprise at having them yet.

One list of rules. (N. B., eating in bedrooms is strictly prohibited. Don't leave crumbs in the bed!)

One probationer, bound to produce herself at stated hours, and liable to be reported at 'the gate' (this is a great hospital phrase;

people are always talking about 'the gate')
if she gets in after hours, or goes out when
she is supposed to be resting.

The view is not exactly charming, being
mostly of chimney-pots, but I've got the home
photographs on the mantelpiece and look at
them instead.

It was strange to go to bed last night and
feel that there wasn't a soul I knew anywhere
near, but I hadn't time to be sentimental
when I woke, for I had to be on duty at seven,
and the wretched cap wouldn't go right for
a long time.

I was lucky at breakfast, for I happened to
sit next to a cheery soul of whom more—much
more—anon. Nurse Adams was so decent,
told me not to be shy or wait for dishes to be
passed. 'It's every one for herself here,' she said.
'Our meals are little more than taking in pro-
visions, we've no time for the social graces!'

However she did find time to be gracious
to me, without the slightest hint of patronage,
and in the kindest manner. And she promised

to look out for me in the sitting-room so I had
something to look forward to, though I was
disappointed to find that I was not going to
start on her ward.

Now wasn't it just grand to think that I
should be sent to the children first? I could
have jumped with joy when I saw the little
darlings. Most of them are getting better,
though there's one mite—with such blue eyes,
Gwen—that made my heart jerk about, she
looks so frail. But more than half of them
were sitting up to say 'Good morning' to the
day nurses, and wish the night nurse good-
bye. They all looked happy, and when they
saw me, they cried, 'A new nurse, look, a new
nurse. Come and tell us your name, Nurse!'

But I wouldn't be tempted, for I knew I
must speak to the Sister, who was at her table
half-way down the ward. She wouldn't be on
duty so early, but we are short-handed in the
children's ward just now, and I hear that she
is not the sort to put all the extra work on
other people while she watches them do it.

I'd heard enough from the others at break-fast-time to know that a pro.'s happiness or misery is in the hands of the ward sister. Well, it's not bliss to work under Sister Matthews, but she is scrupulously fair, and doesn't rake up the past. But she expects the people under her to work, and she doesn't let a thing be out of its place by so much as a hair's breadth. Think what that means to your harum-scarum sister!

Well, we washed the kiddies—beds had been made by the night nurse—and got every-thing ready for the doctor's visit.

I thought there might be some apprehension among the youngsters as the time drew near, but they seemed to look forward to seeing him. I could see eager glances at the clock, and one nipper whose bed gives him a view of the corridor was constantly asked, 'Isn't he com-ing yet?'

I found out part of the reason for this just before he came in, for Curly, who has a broken collar-bone, informed me confidentially that he liked Dr. Norman.

'Do you?' I said.

'Yes, he has sweeties in his pocket.'

I expected to see some fatherly greybeard, but I was surprised when Dr. Norman came to find that he is quite young. The nurses say that he has a brilliant career ahead of him, and that he loves his work. I'm sure he loves his child-patients, for he spends more time in this ward than in any other. His face is thoughtful and pleasant, but not otherwise striking. It was his hands I noticed—the hands of an artist, Gwen. And his slightest touch seemed to soothe the kiddies. I was told to carry round the things he wanted, so I couldn't help seeing them. 'Does it hurt?' he said to Curly.

'It's hurted all the morning, but not while you touch it!'

I wasn't surprised to hear that he plays the violin, really plays it. They say (I'm ashamed to repeat so much gossip, but one can't help hearing it) that he would have made his name as a musician if he hadn't taken up surgery.

He plays for the staff socials every month, so I shall soon get a chance of hearing him.

I expected to be fagged out at the end of the day, and I must admit that I was tired—as tired as you must be of wading through this scrawl—but not so utterly weary as I expected to be. You see, I was so interested.

I could have gone out after seven to-night, but I preferred to stay in and write, because writing to you is the next best thing to hearing you speak, or getting a letter from you. I shall go out to-morrow for a bit, and I'm living for Sunday when we meet at Bloomsbury.

The other young pro. on my ward is quite decent, and very ready to tell me anything. Starting now, I needn't attend lectures till September, but the Sister-Tutor, who coaches for the exams. has given me a list of books that she thinks I should do well to study. I told her I had done some hygiene and physiology at school and she seemed quite pleased.

'That will make the first year's study quite easy for you,' she said. 'Some of the girls who come here have no more idea of physiology than they have of Greek.' She knows our part of the country, Gwen, and has nursed a serious case for Dr. Wilson. It was so nice to hear her speak about him. She knows his wife awfully well, so I shall have to be careful, or dear old Doc. will be hearing of my peccadilloes.

Good night, darling. I know how you felt when you first went to coll. now.

All my love,

Jill.

CHAPTER XII

THE PROGRESS OF A PRO.

Jill's patients were soon well-known to Great Aunt Julia and Gwen, and they followed their recovery with almost as much interest as Jill herself.

There was one little girl who had been sent up from the country and who never had visitors or letters. Jill felt specially sorry for the little mite, and used to do all she could to make her happy. Jill was a great favourite with them all, but little Elsie almost worshipped her, and used to tell Jill all her secrets.

In return she expected to receive Jill's confidence, and asked all sorts of questions about what the nurse did when she was off duty.

'Where are you going to-morrow, nurse?' she asked when Jill told her she would not see her the next day.

'I'm going to see my auntie.'

'Do nurses have aunties?'

'Yes,' laughed Jill, 'why shouldn't they?'

Jill had started attending lectures by this time, and she already stood out from the rest of the pro.'s on account of her energy and zeal. She made mistakes, of course, and she thought more of the patient's feelings than was altogether comfortable for her own, but the Ward Sister said to the Assistant Matron, 'If that girl isn't near the top of the exam. list, I shall be very much surprised. She was more help at the end of a week than some of them are after months on the ward.'

Jill was keenly disappointed when things did go wrong, but she soon found that her own work compared very favourably with that of other young nurses. She never had any trouble in managing her small charges, who were always willing to take their medicine if Nurse Lomax held the cup, and sat patiently under her hands to be washed and dressed.

Her three months with the little ones went

all too quickly. She knew she could not expect to stay in the Children's Ward indefinitely, and was anxious to gain wider experience, a fact which lessened the sorrow of parting from her 'babies'.

'Mind you come in to see us sometimes,' they begged.

Jill never quite made up her mind whether she hated night duty, or whether it was just bearable. That she did not like it goes without saying. At first she was horribly afraid that the patients would be taken worse in the night, but later on she came to take everything as a matter of course. And she always found plenty to do, for she did not spare herself, and was ready to take any pains to add to the comfort of her charges.

She had a little more freedom in the day now, even after she had taken her proper rest time, and she went out quite a lot. Finding that it was not easy to get into the larger hospitals at her age, she had boldly decided to train at a municipal hospital south of the river, but quite close to it. This hospital served a poor and crowded district, and as Jill went to and fro between her work and her aunt's house, she saw a phase of the life of London which was quite new to her, and which helped to make her understand the look on the wan faces of her patients.

'Are you sure, Jill,' said Miss Lomax, 'that you would not rather have done your training in a better district? I don't think it is doing you any harm, but these are depressing scenes by which you are surrounded.'

Jill had been telling her about a little group of sickly children who had been on the tram with her.

'I wouldn't change now if I had the chance to!' said Jill stoutly. 'I think it needs people who haven't got used to such scenes to work among them. I don't take all those slums for granted, as the other people seem to do. And I'm all the keener to undo the ill-effects of such places because I feel so strongly that they simply oughtn't to exist!'

'My dear Jill! You are getting quite an orator! But I'm afraid one nurse can't do much in the way of slum-clearance.'

Jill pulled a newspaper cutting from her bag.

'Please read that, Great Aunt Julia,' she said.

It was a moving article headed, 'A morning with the out-patients'. It described the pathetic rows of waiting patients, clutching cards and bottles, herded together and sitting listlessly till their turn came for seeing the doctor. It showed how the never-ending stream could not even be checked until the people had the air and sunshine of which they were being robbed by the smoky, crowded streets. It showed how the puny children, ailing mothers, and prematurely aged people might find new vigour if they had homes worthy of the name.

It spoke of the darkness of ignorance — of preventable disease; of warped minds and lost innocence, and ended with a moving plea for the light of the sun and the light of knowledge, for the many thousands now living in a two-fold darkness.

'Did this article turn your thoughts to these matters?'

'My thoughts—the things that I am seeing every day make me think, you know—led to that article. I had put some of it into a letter to Gwen, but I took out the sheets again, thinking that I wouldn't trouble the dear child now she is studying so hard. But I didn't destroy them, and after reading another article about a hospital in this paper, I thought I would knock mine into shape and send it along. I was surprised that they printed it, though, I must say.'

'I'm not surprised,' said Miss Lomax. 'You describe those people most vividly, Jill. I seemed to sense the hospital atmosphere as I read about them. Did you get paid for the article?'

'Yes,' said Jill, 'and as I felt I couldn't spend the money, I put it in the box in which money is collected to help patients who need crutches and things after they are discharged.'

'You have very little time for writing, I know,' said Miss Lomax, 'but I think you ought to do more. You are very observant, and you have the power of making your readers see the things and people you are describing.'

'Yes,' said Jill, 'I wanted to make people see those slums and the poor folk who have to live in them. Lots of people never go near them, and those who know they are there just take them for granted. But if I lived in them for fifty years, I should be just as angry at their existence as I am now! Such things simply ought not to be!'

'Well, go on learning and looking and showing others what you see,' said Miss Lomax. 'One little nurse, if she has a pen as fiery as her tongue, and a heart as warm as it can be, will help to educate public opinion, I fancy. You must be sure to show me all your articles, my dear.'

Jill promised to do so, and Miss Lomax read and re-read them all. The old lady visited the hospital and was keenly interested in all that she saw. Like a great many other Londoners, she knew little of the crowded parts of the great city, and she assured Jill that nothing she had written was too strongly worded.

'I hate to think of your living in such surroundings,' she said, 'although I admit that the hospital itself is very different from those dreadful streets. As soon as you show any signs of growing pale there, I shall come and carry you off. But I can guess how much worse things would be for those poor folk without their hospital, and people like you to work in it.'

CHAPTER XIII

THE OUT-PATIENT

'Look in at the dispensary for me as you go off duty, please, Nurse Lomax. They haven't sent that ether I want,' said the Ward Sister to Jill one evening. 'You don't mind, do you?'

'Not a bit, Sister,' said Jill cheerfully. 'I'll run back with it myself, if you like.'

'No, don't bother to do that,' was the reply. 'Let them send it up. You are a little late as it is.'

The dispensary was at the end of the corridor where the out-patients had to wait to see the doctor. The last of a long file had just been handed a bottle as Jill got to the pigeon-hole through which they were served.

'That's the lot, thank goodness,' said the dispenser. 'What a crowd to-night! I'm tired to death.'

'That's why you forgot the ether for my ward then,' said Jill. 'It's wanted at once, please.'

'I'll fly up with it this very minute. I'd better switch on that end light for you, Nurse! The end of the corridor is so dark, and the "Outs" usually leave some souvenirs for us to fall over. Sometimes it's a shopping basket, and sometimes fish and chips.'

'It's a baby this time,' said Jill, '*and* a man! Good gracious! Why ever are you sitting there when every one else has gone home?'

The 'baby' who was in fact a sharp-looking mite of a girl whose age might have been anything from six to ten, blinked at the light and yawned. She had evidently been asleep. The man beside her was huddled on the form, and did not take the slightest interest in the conversation.

'Which is the patient?' asked Jill, looking from one to the other in amazement. She did not know which caused her to wonder more—the shrewdness of the child's face or the helplessness of the man.

' 'E's the *pi*tient!' said the girl shrilly. 'I fitched 'im along, I did, cos muvver got fed up wiv seeing 'im sit about so 'elpless like.'

'What's the matter with him?' asked Jill, trying to see the man's face. He sat with his chin sunk on his chest, his shoulders hunched and his hands lying listlessly in his lap. She had seen the attitude hundreds of times since she came to the hospital—it struck her as the symbol of utter despair when she first saw it—but there was something different about the man which atracted her attention.

She hardly knew what that difference was. From what she could see of the man, he seemed to be dressed in the usual shapeless garments of poverty, garments whose cheap smartness so quickly gave place to shabbiness. The sallowness of the slum-dweller was there, and the grime too. An unkempt beard covered the chin and a twisted handkerchief made a pitiful substitute for a collar, yet the whole effect was not quite that of a street loafer. The man had not always been in that state, and a dim reflection of past manliness hung about him still.

'I dunno what's the matter wiv 'im,' said the sharp child, lowering her voice and glancing at the man out of the corner of her eye, ' 'e don't seem to 'ave no use of his limbs, or his wits either.'

'Is he your father?' asked the dispenser, looking through her little window at the pair.

'No, 'e ain't nothink to do wiv us, reelly. Farver brought 'im 'ome a long time ago, and 'e don't do nothink—just sits all diy like you see 'im now.'

'It's very kind of your father to look after him,' said Jill, 'I suppose he hasn't any money?'

'You bet 'e ain't. And 'e ain't likely to get none, the way 'e goes on. Muvver says she ain't going to put up wiv 'im much longer— 'er nerves will give out if she has to sit looking at him diy after diy!'

'Why didn't you go into the doctor at the

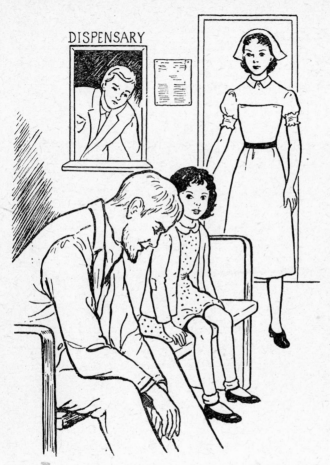

'I dunno what's the matter wiv 'im,' said the sharp
child

right time?' asked Jill. 'I'm afraid you are too late now.'

'I sat aginst that 'ot pipe, and went right off to sleep,' said the girl. 'Farver woke us all up last night, 'e cime in merry and woke us all up and made us dance. 'E ain't 'alf a oner when he gets merry!'

Jill shuddered a little at the hardened slum child. She had seen the gentleness and kindness which abounds among the poor when their neighbours are in trouble, and this contempt for the helpless and admiration of the drunken antics of the father, jarred on Jill all the more because of the youth of the child who showed them.

'I oughtn't to blame her, though,' thought Jill. 'She is what her surroundings have made her.' Then she added aloud, 'I'll take you to the doctor and explain; he may be able to do something for you, although it is so late.'

'Dr. Norman is on to-night,' said the dispenser, 'you need not be afraid of asking him to stretch a point.'

Jill would hardly have dared to trouble the doctor so late in the evening, when she knew that he had already had a hard day, but she hated the thought of the helpless man being left to the mercy of the sharp child and her unfeeling parents. She felt sure that the father had his own reasons for keeping the man at his house, for the way that the child spoke told her that the visitor was considered a nuisance.

'I'd hate any one I knew to be in the hands of such people,' thought Jill. 'But what can the man do? He is dreadfully poor, and evidently quite unable to think for himself.'

The child took the man's arm and he went with her quite mechanically. She was used to looking after him, it seemed.

'Mind the step!' she said shrilly. ' 'E never looks where 'e's goin',' she added to Jill.

'I'm so sorry to trouble you, doctor,' said Jill, 'but I happened to find these two waiting in the corridor. The child who brought the patient had fallen asleep in the warmth, and the poor man was too helpless to make his

way in to see you without being told to come.
I expect the nurses on duty thought that they
were waiting for other patients.'

'Ah!' said the doctor, looking from the
patient to the child, and back to the man again.
The latter stood just where the child put him,
while she, bent on delivering the message
which had been entrusted to her before she
could be told that she had come too late,
gabbled out,

'Please, sir, will you look at 'im, and
muvver says can't nothing be done for 'im for
'e sits about so 'elpless and don't seem to know
what you say to 'im.'

'A relative of yours?' asked the doctor.

'No, sir.'

'Lodger?'

'No, sir.'

'What then?'

'Farver brought 'im 'ome.'

'To work for him?'

'No-o!' (rather doubtfully).

'What for, then?'

'I dunno.'

'What's his name?'

'He ain't got none.'

'Nonsense, child, he must have a name. What does your father call him.'

'Don't call 'im nothink. Jus' sez, "Come on, you!" or "Op orf to bed, mitey!" or what 'tis.'

'And he goes?'

' 'E mostly does what you tells 'im. *I* can manage 'im a treat, I can. Muvver sez I'm a fair caution wiv 'im. Hi, mister, tike yer hat orf when you come in to see the doctor!'

The last remark was addressed to her charge by way of demonstrating her influence over the poor wretch. He had his frowsy cap in his hand, but seemed unaware of the fact, for his shaking hand went to his head at the child's order. He looked confused at finding no cap there, but fully two minutes passed before he realized that he had it in his hand.

Dr. Norman looked at the child with increasing dislike. Jill had never seen him give a child such a look before.

'Do you know the way to the porter's lodge?' he asked her quietly.

'The gite? I knows the gite all right.'

'Then go and wait there till I bring the man back to you. You can sit by the fire, if you are good.'

The girl went off willingly enough, and Dr. Norman spoke to the porter on the telephone.

'I've sent a child to you to wait till I come out with a patient that she will take home. Let her talk if she is inclined to, and find out anything you can about the man who came with her.'

'That's unorthodox,' he said, turning to Jill with a smile after he had hung up the receiver, 'but this is no common case. I can see you are interested, Nurse, so I am going to ask you to stay in case I should want help.'

'I'd like to,' said Jill, simply.

The doctor drew a form towards him, and

picked up a pen to note down the usual information.

'Name—unknown. Address—can get that from our too-sharp young friend at the gate. Age—say twenty-eight, but might be younger. Nature of illness—ah, let's look at him.'

He turned to the patient and sounded his heart, asked him to walk across the room, to move a chair, to find a page in a book. All these things were done very slowly and awkwardly, and in a listless way. Yet there was a dull sense of wonder about it all, too.

'What's your name?' asked the doctor curtly.

Jill realized that he wanted to take the man by surprise. He might be malingering, of course. He might be playing a part, but if so, he was playing it remarkably well.

He looked vacantly at the doctor.

'Tell me your name,' said Dr. Norman sharply.

The man pressed his hand over his forehead, and then shook his head despairingly.

'Gone,' he said. 'Gone since the darkness came.'

'What darkness?'

'This,' said the man, waving his hands about vaguely. 'It's all round me. Can't you see it? I can *feel* it.'

He closed his hands slowly as if he were shutting them on to some actual object, then opened them again and let them fall limply to his side.

'Is it dark with the child?' asked the doctor.

'Yes, the darkness is all round her. I'm glad she's gone. I don't like her.'

'Then you don't want to go back with her?'

'No!' There was a fearful energy in the way he brought out the word. 'The men, the woman, the girl—they weren't there till the darkness came. They help to keep it dark, they shut out the light.'

'Where were you before the darkness came?' asked the doctor. 'Don't hurry, think, and then tell me.'

Again that despairing shake of the head.

'Where is your home?'

'With her!' A look at the door by which the child had gone out, and a sigh.

'No, no, your old home, I mean.'

'But that's before the darkness came.' He spoke reprovingly as if to say, 'You know I can't tell you about that.'

'I'll look at your head now, please. I won't hurt you.'

Jill helped the patient to a chair. It was the first time she had touched him, and the man started and drew back. Then he turned away and covered his face with his hands.

'What have I done?' asked Jill, turning to the doctor in dismay.

'I think you have touched some chord connected with his past. It may be the uniform—he may have known a nurse—or your features may recall some one that he knows. That is hopeful, I think, but don't obtrude on his notice. Stand back, please, Nurse, but don't go away.'

He ran his fingers over the man's head.

Jill saw the patient flinch as he reached a spot over the right eye. The doctor felt the movement and examined the place more closely.

He nodded and said, 'A severe blow. I expected something of the sort. It has caused him to lose his memory and made him almost childish.'

'What will you do with him, Doctor? Must he go back to that dreadful place? I'm sure it is not fit for him to be there.'

'He had better stay here. I'll X-ray that wound to-morrow. No doubt the people he was with will be glad to get rid of him for a time.'

'Is there any hope of his recovery?' asked Jill.

'Oh, I think so! I quite think so! Once the pressure is relieved and he has time to get over the shock. There must have been severe shock to bring about this condition. The wound itself would scarcely account for it.'

He picked up the telephone again.

'Porter, tell the child to go home, please. The patient must stay here for a time. Tell her to send her father or her mother to me at once.'

He waited to hear that the child had understood the message and had gone to deliver it, and then said to Jill, 'I don't for a moment think they will come. We shall never hear of them again.'

'But aren't they responsible for him?' ventured Jill.

'Responsibility doesn't mean much to some people,' said Dr. Norman. 'My own opinion is that this man was the dupe of the child's father, and was mixed up in some shady business with him. He's of no use to any one now, but they kept him close for a time so that he shouldn't give the game away.'

'He can't tell much,' said Jill.

'But they would never know how much he might tell. I think from the way the child spoke that the mother sent him here without the father's knowledge. He is probably away on some errand of his own, and the woman took advantage of his absence.'

'Is there anything more I can do?' asked Jill as the porters came to take the man to the receiving ward.

'No, thank you, nurse. I'm sorry you were kept. The night duty folk will do all there is to do. Don't let me keep you.'

Jill heard that the man was being taken to the ward next to the one in which she was working, and she made up her mind to keep informed of the strange patient's progress. She had never felt so touched by a case before. The man's helplessness went to her heart, and she revolted at the idea of his being the tool of some scoundrel such as Dr. Norman had described.

'I'll ask Dr. Norman about him later on,' she determined, 'he will be able to tell me much more than the nurses, and I'm sure he won't mind my asking. He was so decent to-night, and talked to me in quite a friendly way. I'm sure he is keen to do all he can for that poor fellow.'

CHAPTER XIV

STILL IN THE DARK

Jill had no chance of asking about the strange patient for a few days, for she herself took a bad cold, and was sent off duty by the Sister.

When she went back to her ward, another nurse was away ill, and there was so much to do that she was too tired to talk at meal times, and spent nearly all her off-duty time in bed.

Dr. Norman was away; he went from the hospital while Jill was ill, and she did not venture to ask the other doctors about her protégé. She did not know what to call him, and had not mentioned her share in his being taken in for treatment.

Still, she did not forget him, and when she went to the ward on an errand, she looked along the two rows of beds to see if she could recognize him.

She saw no patient in the least like the one who had interested her so much, and she had no time to ask about the man whose bed had a screen round it, even if she had felt bold enough to do so.

'Perhaps he was fetched away after all,' thought Jill. 'Those people may have been anxious not to let him out of their reach. However, it's really no business of mine, and I don't want to excite remark by inquiring about him.'

Her only hope of getting to know the facts lay in the knowledge that Dr. Norman had seen how interested she was, and she was anxious to get a chance of speaking to him when he returned to the hospital.

She got it sooner than she expected. The doctor had spent the day in the hospital but had not been in her ward, and when Jill got on a tram to go to her aunt's she found herself followed by the doctor.

He smiled and took a seat beside her.

'I came out of the gate behind you,' he said, 'and I hoped you would be going my way, as I wanted to tell you about your patient.'

Jill knew at once whom he meant.

'I speak as though you had charge of him, but I sent him to another ward, didn't I? That was partly because of the effect you had on him the other night, and partly because I wanted to have him under my own eye.'

'How is he getting on?' asked Jill.

'Very well indeed, up to a certain point. By the way, you wouldn't recognize him, Nurse. He's had a shave, and he looks like a different man. I thought he wasn't one of the natives!'

'Do you mean that he is a foreigner?' asked Jill, who was apt to take things very literally.

'No, no! I meant that he didn't belong to this district. Though, by the way, he may not be English. He speaks like an educated man, but there's the slightest trace of an accent about his speech that isn't like any provincial English that I know, and I can usually place a man.'

'Scottish or Irish, perhaps,' said Jill.

'No, if it's anything, it is the merest tinge of American accent, but scarcely noticeable, if it is.' Jill turned her head to look at the traffic, and scolded herself for the momentary flush that came to her cheek.

'He's had the X-ray——' she began.

'Yes, and the operation. Came through that splendidly. I operated the day after he came in.'

'And can he give any account of himself?' asked Jill.

'No, but his manner is changed. He has the bearing of a gentleman now. You can't imagine anything more remote from the broken-down wretch that you found in the corridor.'

'I should like to see him,' said Jill, after a little hesitation. 'Finding him as I did made me very interested in him, as you know.'

'Ah, but I don't want you to see him yet. You must wait my time.'

'I didn't mean to talk to him,' said Jill, flushing. 'I meant I should like to look at him as I passed down the ward, on some pretext.'

'See here, Nurse, I don't even want you to do that! I have a special reason for telling you about him. I believe I am going to want your help. You remember that night in the out-patients' department, how he started when you touched him, and then covered his face with his hands.'

'Yes,' said Jill wonderingly.

'I thought then that he had some past association with a nurse, which might help him to recall the past. But he takes no notice of the nurses on the ward, so I have to conclude that it was some personal trait of yours which stirred a passing memory.'

'Then what do you want me to do?' asked Jill.

'I want you to wait till he is stronger, and

then I will take you to see him when I go round the wards. You shall come one morning when you are off duty, wearing mufti, for the uniform may only confuse him.'

Jill pondered over this for a time.

'What would you like me to wear?' she asked.

'Something quiet—not that I imagine you are ever very flamboyant, nurse!' he said with a smile. 'But something ordinary—so that the clothes don't distract his attention.'

'It's a very interesting case,' said Jill.

'It *is* an interesting case,' said the doctor. 'I am very keen on getting that man fit again, I can tell you. I am sure he is a thoroughly decent fellow, and I am seldom mistaken in my estimate of a character.'

'I shall be glad to do anything I can,' said Jill. 'He was so helpless when I found him that I couldn't help wanting to take care of him.'

'Well, don't let him see you till I take you to the ward,' said Dr. Norman. 'I sit with him sometimes in the evening, and try to get him to talk, but he is rather weak yet, and certainly not ready for a shock.'

'Will seeing me be a shock for him?' asked Jill with a twinkle in her eye. It was impossible for her to feel in awe of the man she had seen romping with the kiddies in the children's ward.

'Not for personal reasons. He ought to be delighted to have such a visitor,' said the doctor, 'but if my theory is true, and you can bring back the past, that will be a shock for him at first. But it's only a theory, mind, and you must not be disappointed if it doesn't have any effect.'

'He'll be able to work now, even if he can't remember who he is, I suppose,' said Jill.

'He's got a splendid constitution and he is pulling up remarkably well. He's perfectly sane too, not the slightest hint of mental derangement. I should say he is a man to make his way in the world, even if he has to start right from the bottom.'

'He is at the bottom now, poor fellow,' said

Jill. 'No home, no friends, no clothes but the ones he stood up in. You never heard any more of the people he was with, I take it.'

'No, the child let out the name of the street, but she didn't give her name or the number of the house. We could comb out the street, of course, if it were to his interest for those people to be found.'

'But it isn't,' said Jill quickly.

'No, I don't think it is. He's all right here for a time. There is nothing to be gained by finding out those people. If he gets well, he won't want them, and if he doesn't I must get him into some institution where he will be well cared for.'

Jill's thoughts flew to Cyrus's hundred pounds.

'I've got some money, doctor,' she said, 'not much, but enough to give him a start, that was left me by a relative under circumstances that make me unwilling to spend it on myself. I don't think it could be put to a better use than helping this poor man.'

'The circumstances are exceptional,' said the doctor. 'Well, he's your patient, by right of discovery, and you shall certainly know if you can help him financially. I may want him sent to a quiet place in the country, a farmhouse or something of that sort. He's better by himself, I fancy. I have told them to keep the screen round his bed for that reason.'

'My people have a farm,' Jill began.

'See here now,' said the doctor, 'your people can't turn the house into a convalescent home for all your patients! Your heart is a little too big, I'm thinking!'

The rebuke was so gently given that Jill met it with a smile. 'I get off here,' she said. 'Thank you so much for telling me all about him. I was anxious for news.'

Gwen was on holiday, and both she and Miss Lomax were very interested in Jill's account of the strange patient.

Jill could not praise the doctor too highly, and Gwen began to tease her about him.

'I believe our sober-sides is falling in love

with the doctor!' she cried. 'I've been hearing about this wonderful doctor ever since she went to the hospital.'

'I'm in love with his skill!' said Jill stoutly. 'I'd give anything to be able to do the miracles he does! And his patience! I simply haven't words to describe his patience and his gentle, sympathetic manner.'

'There she goes!' cried Gwen. 'This is a bad case! Our Jill is hard hit! Does he return your affections, Jill?'

'I hope he gives me credit for more sense!' cried Jill. 'You don't understand, Gwen. I'm no more to him than any other piece of hospital furniture. He happens to have a special occasion for me just now, as he might want some particular instrument for any other case. The only difference is that I shan't be sterilized when he has done with me!'

'I should think not!' cried Gwen. 'We can't have our old Jill boiled! Her cheeks are hot enough already!'

'You shouldn't tease her so, Gwen,' said

Miss Lomax, looking at Jill's bright face and
wondering how much of the interest she took
in the doctor was purely professional.

'Oh, I don't mind,' said Jill. 'The poor
child must have some amusement when she
is on holiday, mustn't she?'

'Won't you be scared to death when he
takes you to be looked at by the strange man?'
asked Gwen.

'Why should I?' asked Jill. 'The patient
won't know that I've come for that purpose.
Dr. Norman often takes visitors round. The
only part I shan't like will be explaining the
whole business to the other nurses on that
ward.'

'I hope that the experiment is a success,'
said the old lady. 'We shall want to know all
about it, Jill.'

'I'll tell you all that happens,' said the girl.
'I'm so keen on the poor man getting his
memory back. Dr. Norman says he is changed
already by the operation; he seems like
another man.'

'I can see Jill going down to fame as the woman who restored a long-lost husband to his weeping wife,' said Gwen.

Jill gave a little start. 'I hadn't thought about his having friends,' she said. 'Being so lost and helpless, I thought of him as quite alone—for you can't count those people who had him before. But, of course, there may be near relatives who have spent anxious months wondering what has befallen him.'

She was so silent after this speech that Gwen had to rally her again.

'I'm going to be jealous!' she declared. 'I simply haven't got a sister these days! She has made herself over body and soul to that wretched hospital, and she can't think of anything else!'

'Well, I must think of going back to it then!' said Jill, 'for my time is up. I've never been reported late yet, and I don't want to start now!'

'I'll come to the bus-stop with you,' said Gwen. 'I wish it wasn't such a horrid journey.

This end is bad enough, but that tram ride at the other end—ugh!'

'I'm nearly sure to see some of the nurses going back on the tram,' said Jill. 'It's not so bad if you have some one to talk to. I'm too tired to read on the way back.'

'I hope you are not doing too much, Jill,' said Great Aunt Julia. 'It's a hard life for any one who feels so strongly about the things she sees as you do.'

'I wouldn't change it for the world!' declared Jill. 'I'm longing for my week at home later on, but I love the hospital. It has taught me such a lot!'

'And this is the girl who thought that she couldn't be spared from home!' said Great Aunt Julia.

'Don't you know that you told me that I wanted some of my corners rubbed off?' replied Jill merrily. 'You urged me to leave home, you know!'

'And did I do right?' said the old lady, with a little tender smile which was often on her lips when she looked at Jill.

'You did!' said Jill decidedly. 'Dad is managing better than he ever did when I was at home; Freddie is turning out a steady fellow and a good farmer; Emmeline is by way of being a model housekeeper and things are brighter altogether than they have been for years! They are all the better for not having me to meddle with them!'

'I don't know how we should have got on when Dad was ill without your meddling, as you call it,' said Gwen. 'I never get a letter from home that doesn't say how they are missing you! After all this time they still haven't got used to doing without you.'

'Little flatterer!' said Jill. 'Great Aunt Julia tries to rub my corners off, and you insist on doing your best to make me vain. But look at the time! I must run!'

'Good night, my dear!' said her aunt. 'There was some selfishness in my plan of bringing you to London, you know. I wanted to have you near me.'

Jill blew her a kiss, and the two girls ran to the bus-stop. Luckily Jill had not long to wait, and she was soon climbing into the bus which took her the first part of her way.

'Go straight home, childie!' she called to Gwen. 'Little girls oughtn't to be out so late all by themselves!'

Gwen waved her latch-key—such liberties had Great Aunt Julia come to allow her nieces!—by way of answer, and stood watching until the bus which carried off her beloved Jill was out of sight.

'I don't want her to fall in love with her doctor,' she said. 'I want to keep her for myself a little longer yet!'

CHAPTER XV

THE PATIENT

The darkness of which he had spoken to the doctor no longer troubled the unknown patient. His perplexity had vanished and he was at peace. Dimly he was aware that he had no reason to distrust the doctor and nurses, and that he was more at ease than he had been for a long time. His cares receded into the background of his thoughts; they were like a dream that had been—a dream that he knew would not return.

He lay, clean and comfortable—that was much after the life he had been forced to lead—and without a care in the world. He could not have said how long he had been there, for time had lost its meaning for him.

He vaguely recognized the doctor, and even seemed to look forward to his visits, perhaps because he was associated with the improvement in his circumstances.

He knew he was in bed; he knew that people came to him from some outer world beyond his screen, but he had not the slightest curiosity as to what went on there. He dozed a good deal, but there were times when he lay for hours staring straight in front of him, but passively, and not with any inquiry in his eyes.

He had become accustomed to the periodic visits of the nurses, and helped them where he could by moving as they wished him to. He took the food that was given him, but seemed to eat mechanically. And he never spoke unless he was asked a question. He would answer briefly to any inquiry about his food, or tell them how he felt—'Quite comfortable. I can rest now,' was his usual answer.

The doctor had strictly forbidden the nurses to ask him any personal questions, and had said that perfect quiet was his chief need. But the doctor himself chatted to him on general matters, the weather, the news, and so on, and watched keenly for any signs of interest in the topics he brought up.

It was difficult to know how much the patient realized about his position. He had certainly grown accustomed to the hospital routine, and even showed a faint surprise at any deviation from it. But he made no comment and was in everything so passive that it was at times difficult to realize that he was conscious.

His physical condition mended steadily, and he was allowed to sit up in bed for a time every day. He seemed to take a little pleasure in this, perhaps realizing that it meant he was growing stronger.

He slept well, and did not talk in his sleep, to the disappointment of the doctor, who had hoped to learn something of his past by this means. His condition was satisfactory, however, in that his mental state was ideal for recuperation. His recovery would undoubtedly have been hindered if he had been restless or anxious, but there was something almost uncanny in his detachment.

The doctor tried the experiment of leaving papers and books on his locker, but he made no attempt to read them. He looked at them meaningly, but without speaking, when the nurse came to him later on, as much as to say, 'There is something that is no concern of mine. Aren't you going to take it away?'

Dr. Norman saw him frequently, and observed him very closely. The patient always turned his head towards him when he came round the screen, and seemed to expect that he would want to look at the old wound.

An intelligent child of two might have grown used to the hospital life in the way he did, and been content to live in the present without troubling about either past or future. But the child would have prattled about home and wanted to run about the ward as he grew stronger.

The child, too, would have wanted amusing,

but the patient never complained of weariness, never appeared to want any diversion.

By way of preparing him for the great experiment of which he hoped so much, Dr. Norman occasionally took one of the other doctors, or a nurse out of uniform, with him when he went to see the patient. But beyond a faint surprise at this irregular proceeding, to which, however, he showed no personal objection, the visitors made no impression on him.

The rest of the medical staff regarded the case as hopeless, and thought that it was extremely improbable that his brain would ever function normally again. They agreed that the head wound in itself was not serious, and that the operation had undoubtedly removed the pressure and brought about a great improvement in the man's condition. But they thought that a great shock, or severe distress of mind for a long period had impaired the tissues. They thought it was a case for a mental hospital, as the man was then incapable of looking after himself, though how much of that was due to physical weakness remained to be seen.

His expression was not vacant, but was habitually drowsy. His state was most like that of a person rousing from sleep but not fully awake, but with the difference that it was a permanent state, and he never roused beyond a certain point. Waking or sleeping, his face bore the same restful look, and when Dr. Norman contrasted it with the distress with which he had spoken of 'the darkness' on the night when he first came to the hospital, he felt that he had every reason for being satisfied with the result of the operation.

The doctor ventured to use the word darkness in the course of conversation, introducing it naturally and without emphasis. He obviously connected it with the darkness of night, but no longer attached any symbolical meaning to it, as he had done when he spoke about it in the out-patients' department.

Dr. Norman had found out more about the

people who had sheltered him, with the help of the police. The father of the sharp child was a race-course frequenter and although he had never been convicted, the police kept their eyes on him. He was a clever man and the police-sergeant to whom the doctor spoke thought it highly probable that he had had his own reasons for taking charge of the patient.

'Perhaps it would be as well if you said nothing about him, Doctor. We can lay our hands on this chap whenever we want him, and if he doesn't know we are keeping an eye on him, we shall be better able to make use of anything your patient can tell us later on.'

'I don't think he will be able to tell you anything,' said the doctor. 'That part of his life will probably be wiped out of his memory as completely as his former life was when he first came to us.'

'A strange thing, sir!' observed the sergeant.

'The hospital authorities usually want to

know who is responsible for a patient, but I have resumed responsibility in this case, and to be quite frank, I don't want to send the man back to his old associates. I'm sure he deserves a better fate.'

'You'll let me know if your man can tell us anything about the people down yonder?' said the sergeant, as he said good-bye.

'I certainly will,' said the doctor.

CHAPTER XVI

THE EXPERIMENT

Jill was glad when the doctor told her that he thought the time had come when he might safely show her to the patient, in the hope that she might touch some memory and help him to remember his former life.

'I shall tell him that I am bringing a visitor who is interested in him, and who wants to help him when he leaves the hospital,' he said. 'So far no one has mentioned the fact that he is not staying here indefinitely, as he seems to think he is. The screen is still round his bed, so he has not had the chance of seeing how the other patients come and go.'

'Am I to talk to him?' asked Jill.

'Only the merest commonplaces,' said the doctor. 'We shall soon see if you have the effect on him that I am hoping to see. I want you to observe him closely, as I shall do, of course, so that we can compare notes afterwards. I am always on the watch for anything that seems to interest him. If this clue fails we must try to find others.'

'He didn't see me very clearly that night,' remarked Jill thoughtfully. 'He stood with his chin on his neck as you no doubt remember. He never looked up at me once, and I came from behind to help him to the chair. It was when I touched him that he started back.'

'Then shake hands with him when you see him,' said the doctor promptly, 'and please take that anxious look off your face, Nurse. I want the whole thing to appear quite casual.'

'Sorry,' said Jill, 'but so much depends upon it, that I can't help feeling anxious on the poor man's account.'

'A great deal *does* depend on it,' agreed the doctor, 'but not upon you personally. Don't let it worry you.'

Jill waited in the ward while the doctor

went round the screen. She could hear his voice as he greeted the patient.

'Good morning. How are you to-day? You look heaps better!'

The patient's answer was inaudible, but it seemed to be satisfactory, for the doctor went on, 'I've brought a visitor to see you — a lady who is hoping to be able to be of use to you. You don't mind seeing her?'

After a brief pause the doctor came to Jill and beckoned to her to come out into the corridor.

'He is much brighter this morning. I'm decidedly hopeful! Just chat casually; I'll tell you when to go.'

They walked back to the screened bed together. Jill's heart thumped painfully. She scolded herself for being so much affected by the thought of the coming interview.

'It's a mere nothing!' she said to herself. 'No more than stopping to speak to any other patient who wants cheering up.'

Dr. Norman seemed to guess her thoughts,

for he smiled encouragingly and said, 'I shan't keep you long!'

'I mustn't let him think I am a little fool!' thought Jill. 'I'd value his good opinion more than that of any one else in the whole hospital.'

The other nurses on the ward were very interested in the experiment, of which they had only just heard.

They kept within sight of the screen as far as their duties permitted, and were evidently anxious for the success of Doctor Norman's test. The Ward Sister came with the doctor, but stopped short at the screen. The doctor led the way, with lips set, and a hopeful gleam in his eye.

'Here she is!' he said to the patient.

Jill gave one look at the figure on the bed. The face that was turned towards her had very little resemblance to the one she had seen in the corridor, even allowing for the fact that she now saw it clearly for the first time.

It was a keen face, and would have been a very intelligent one but for the habitual look of drowsiness. It was pale and thin, but that was not the reason why Jill gave a painful gasp as she looked at it.

She tried to speak, but the words would not come. She moistened her dry lips with her tongue, and tried again, but the words she so badly wanted to utter refused to pass her lips.

Dr. Norman, intent on his patient, did not notice her distress. The man showed a greater interest than he had done in anything he had seen since he came to the hospital. A new expression crept over the passive face, and the doctor said to Jill, but without turning to look at her, so intent was he on the man in the bed, 'Speak to him, Nurse.'

He was not prepared for the word that came in answer to his request. Instead of the formal 'Good morning!' or some ordinary remark about his health, there came a half-strangled cry of 'Cyrus!' and a dull thud behind him told him that the nurse he had brought to arouse the dormant faculties of his patient had collapsed on the floor.

Full of wonder at this strange event, but still intent on following every movement of every muscle of his patient's face, he called, 'Sister, see to Nurse, please!' and bent over the bed just in time to hold the man, who after an incredulous cry of 'Jill!' dropped back on his pillows.

'No doubt of its success!' said the doctor to himself. 'She has most certainly reminded him of some one that he knew. Now to follow this up.'

He settled the man comfortably on the pillows, and stood so that he could not see Jill, who was being carried away by the Sister and one of the nurses.

'Rest for a minute, old man. You shall tell me all about her presently.'

'It *was* Jill Lomax,' he said, 'wasn't it? Do tell me! And ask her to come back.'

'She shall come back presently,' said the doctor. 'She is not quite well. Will you promise me to lie quite still here with your eyes shut, while I go to look after her?'

'Yes!' He shut his eyes at once. 'You will be quick, won't you?'

'Ever so quick, and I'll bring her back as soon as she feels well enough to come.' He kept his gentle hand on the man's shoulder while he was speaking. 'You can tell me your name now, can't you?'

'Didn't you know it? Cyrus J. Lomax.'

The doctor beamed with delight. 'That's fine! Now just rest there until I bring her back. Don't forget, keep your eyes shut, and rest.'

He beckoned to the nurse who was still in the ward to keep an eye on the patient, and hurried to the little room off the main ward where he knew he would find Jill.

She was lying on the bed, pale and trembling, but quite conscious. The doctor went to her and felt her pulse.

He was still unaware of the fact that Jill had recognized his patient, not having understood her cry.

'You must have been overworking lately,

young woman,' he said. 'I'm going to ward
you for a month's rest! You should have told
me you were not feeling fit.'

'It's not that, Doctor,' cried Jill, sitting up
in spite of the Sister's attempt to stop her.
'I can hardly believe it yet myself, but your
unknown patient is my cousin, who has been
missing since Easter.'

'What's his name?' asked the doctor
quickly.

'Cyrus J. Lomax,' said Jill with a sob.

CHAPTER XVII

EXPLANATIONS

'Your cousin?' said Dr. Norman. 'Then why didn't you tell me so before? No wonder you were so agitated.'

'But I didn't know,' cried Jill. 'Think how different he looks now! And I didn't see him properly that night in the out-patients' department. He never once looked straight at me.'

The doctor paced excitedly about the room.

'By Jove! What a coincidence! No wonder he started when you touched him! Why ever didn't I follow that up then? He might have got his memory back straight away.'

He took another turn or two about the room talking eagerly, but as much to himself as to Jill.

'I don't know, though! I doubt it—he hadn't had the operation then. I don't think

I did far wrong after all. But do tell me more about him, if you feel well enough, that is.'

Jill took a drink of water, which the Sister offered her and said, 'I'm quite all right now. So sorry that I flopped down like that, but it was rather a shock. I hadn't the least idea that I should recognize him, though I have been very interested all along, as you know.'

'Yes, yes,' said the doctor, 'do go on, Nurse.'

'He's a distant cousin,' Jill went on. 'He comes from America. We didn't know anything about him until last Easter, when he looked us up. He hasn't any relatives in America, and wanted to get to know the English branch of the family.

'He stayed with us a few weeks, and one morning we found that he had disappeared in the night. Nothing was missing, in fact, he left money behind him—the money, by the way, that I told you I wanted to use for your unknown patient! We never heard another word of him, though we had parted on the best of terms with him the night before, and he had actually accepted, apparently with great pleasure, an invitation to come to London on a visit to my Great Aunt.'

Dr. Norman followed every word of her story closely.

'Most remarkable! Most remarkable!' he cried. 'I have never heard such a strange story in my life! He may bless his stars that the sharp child brought him here, and that you found him in the corridor that night.'

'You will let me see him again?' said Jill. 'I think he recognized me, and if so he will wonder where I am.'

'I promised to take you back as soon as you felt well enough,' said the doctor. 'He certainly did recognize you, and he was able to tell me his name. So you see our experiment is an undoubted success. I will just speak to him before I send you to him.'

He went back with Jill to the screen, left her there and said to Cyrus, 'All right now, Mr. Lomax?'

'Oh, I'm all right, but what about Jill?' replied an eager voice. 'Have you brought her? Is she better?'

'Yes, here she is,' said the doctor, turning away. He motioned to Jill to take his place, and she went straight to the bed, and, in defiance of all hospital rules—how could she remember them at such a time?—sat on the bed to put her arm round his shoulder.

For a few minutes neither spoke. Jill looked happily at him but with a sigh for his thin, wasted cheeks. Cyrus feasted his eyes on the glowing face of his cousin, and was content.

'How did I get here?' he asked.

'I don't know yet,' said Jill, 'but you are in the hospital where I am learning to be a nurse, and you will soon be well now.'

'A nurse? But how can they spare you from the farm?'

'Oh, quite well,' said Jill. 'They will be so glad when they hear that I have found you.'

'I didn't mean to go away,' said Cyrus after a pause. 'They took me!'

An anxious look came over his face, and Jill hastened to soothe him.

'Never mind that now. You shall tell me by and by. Everything is quite all right now.'

'I shall see you often? You won't go away?'

'I will stay as long as the doctor will let me to-day. I am not on duty till to-morrow morning. I work in the next ward. I am sure they will let me come and see you very often.'

'It's good to see you again.'

'You poor dear! You have had such a dreadful time! But it is all over! Now all you have to do is to get well as soon as you can.'

'Jill, were you angry when I went away?'

'Of course not!'

'Were you sorry? I hoped—you would think of me sometimes, when I found that they were taking me away.'

Jill flushed. 'Could you really think of me at such a time?'

'I thought of you all the time. Then the blows came, and I can't remember what happened after that. I nearly got away, but they caught me again.'

'You're getting tired, Cousin Cyrus,' said Jill. 'I mustn't let you talk too much, but tell me, dear, did you see two men skulking at the gate after you went upstairs that night?'

'Yes,' said Cyrus, 'they signalled to me, and I went down. One of them came over on the boat with me; I knew him to speak to, though he was no friend of mine. I could see he was a slippery customer as soon as I set eyes on him.'

'His name was Seddons and he was called "Flash Jack",' said Jill, as he paused.

'That's right. Jill, you know everything! Well, he told me that he was in trouble, and asked me to help a fellow-countryman. He vowed he'd burgle the house if I didn't help him. I didn't want you frightened, so I said I would go in for my pocket-book. But as I went downstairs again I remembered that they were two to one, and they might take all I had.'

'So you tossed a hundred pounds, sealed up in an envelope with my name written on it, behind the books on the shelf in the little room over the porch,' put in Jill softly to help him out.

'Your notes, Jill. I meant you to have them all along. I put them in that envelope the first night I came to the farm, meaning to *make* you take them some way or another. The fellows set upon me as soon as I came down, and dragged me away.'

Dr. Norman came humming round the screen. Jill had just time to scramble off the bed before his smiling face looked down on the two of them.

'Well?' he said. 'Now you know all about it! Nurse Lomax, go out for a walk or a ride or a game of marbles or whatever diversion you usually take on your off-duty days! Mr. Lomax, go to sleep!'

'Certainly, Doctor!' said Cyrus. 'I'll be glad to obey orders. When shall I see my cousin again?'

'If she comes in about seven, and dodges into the ward when Sister is not looking, she can stay with you for half an hour,' said the doctor. 'She's a splendid stimulant! I can recommend her with confidence!'

He patted Jill's shoulder as he spoke, and thanked her for the help she had given him.

'She's a stimulant that a man can't have too much of!' said Cyrus, as he settled himself to obey the doctor's orders.

CHAPTER XVIII

TELLING THE NEWS

'Thank goodness I'm not on duty to-day!' thought Jill, as she walked out of the hospital. 'I can't realize that it is true, for I feel just as if I had been roused out of a very vivid dream. I should do all sorts of mad things if I had to start work now.'

She went straight to the nearest post-office, and wired to her father, 'Cousin Cyrus found; am writing. Jill.' and then took a tram towards Bloomsbury. By the time she had changed on to the bus for the second part of the journey, she felt a little more collected.

'Dad will be pleased, I'm sure,' she thought, 'and Great Aunt Julia and Gwen will be delighted. They were so interested in my unknown patient that they will be all the more pleased that he should turn out to be

Cyrus. And Emmy and Fred will be ready enough to acknowledge that there is no blame attaching to him for his abrupt departure.'

It was as well that Jill was so lost in her own thoughts that she had no time to look at her fellow passengers, who cast many interested looks at her glowing face.

Jill almost ran along her aunt's street, and she gave such a smart rat-tat at the door that Sarah came rushing up the kitchen stairs to see what was the matter.

'Bless me, Miss Jill!' she said, 'you gave me quite a turn! I thought it was one of those nasty telegrams that mostly bring bad news. But you look as if you had good news to tell.'

'I have,' said Jill, 'the lost cousin is found; he's a patient at my hospital.'

'To think of that now!' said Sarah. 'Trust you to find him, Miss Jill! I'd back you against any four other girls any day of the week.'

Jill smiled an acknowledgement of this compliment, and passed on to the little morn-

ing-room where she knew she would find
Great Aunt Julia.

'You're late, Jill,' said Miss Lomax. 'I
expected you nearly an hour ago.'

'Dr. Norman wanted me,' said Jill. 'He
showed me to the patient who had lost his
memory.'

'I hope you did him good.'

'*I* got a shock,' said Jill, trying not to let
her face betray her.

'Why?' asked the old lady abruptly.

'Because he is—Cousin Cyrus!'

'What!' cried Great Aunt Julia. 'Do you
know what you are saying, child, or are you
talking nonsense?'

'I'm talking sober fact,' Jill assured her.
'You can imagine how surprised I was. It
knocked me out, in fact.'

'Knocked you out?' repeated the old lady
wonderingly.

'Yes, I fainted. Flopped right down on the
floor as soon as I recognized him. Silly,
wasn't it?'

'Did he know you?'

'Yes, and he was a bit flabbergasted. Seeing me brought back all he had forgotten, you see. He could tell the doctor his name then.'

'But how can this strange man be Cousin Cyrus?' said the old lady. 'It's a mystery to me, Jill.'

'I'm not clear about the details myself yet,' replied Jill, 'but it really is Cousin Cyrus! I talked to him for a few minutes after I got over that silly faint. I've never done such a thing before, I assure you, and don't intend to do it again—and I can see him to-night for half an hour.'

'When can I see him?' said Great Aunt Julia.

'To-morrow is visiting day,' said Jill. 'I expect Dr. Norman will let you see him. I'll find out when I get back to the hospital and send you a card.'

'I can hardly believe it,' said Great Aunt Julia.

'What!' cried Great Aunt Julia. 'Do you know what you are saying?'

'I was like that at first,' said Jill.

'To think that he should come to your hospital.'

'We owe that to you,' Jill reminded her.

'How?'

'You advised me to start my training now, didn't you?'

'That made no difference to Cyrus.'

'Oh, but it did! If he hadn't seen me there, he might never have recovered his memory.'

'Ah, yes, I see your point. Very well, then, I may take a little credit in the matter. But it was Jill who did it again. If you want a thing done well, "let Jill do it".'

'So much was pure coincidence,' said Jill, 'for I hardly ever see an out-patient, and so much was due to Dr. Norman's skill and untiring interest, that I really can't claim any credit in the matter. But I am glad to have played a part in it, of course.'

'You must let your father know,' said Miss Lomax.

'I have wired to him, and I'll write after lunch.'

'How much longer must Cyrus stay in hospital?' asked Miss Lomax. 'He is much better, isn't he?'

'I should say he will be fit for discharge in another week or so. He should pull up rapidly now. But I don't know whether he could stand the journey.'

'Not much of a journey,' said Great Aunt Julia.

'Eh?' said Jill.

'He can have a taxi from door to door! That shouldn't tire him very much. I will fetch him myself.'

'Oh,' said Jill, colouring, 'you mean to have him here. I was thinking of his going home to the farm.'

'He has promised to pay me a visit,' said Miss Lomax, 'and now that he is in London, I should not think of letting him go away without staying with me. I expect he will fall in with the plan readily enough.'

'No doubt,' said Jill.

'I don't think he will be in any very tremendous hurry to leave London,' she went on, watching Jill closely as she spoke.

'Probably not,' said Jill, swinging the tassel of the cord which looped back the curtain. 'He's sure to have lots of business to attend to after all this time. Dad will send on his letters. They have all been put by carefully for him.'

Jill had recovered her composure by this time, and was her old nonchalant self.

'I can't think how you didn't recognize him when you saw him first,' said Great Aunt Julia.

'I didn't see his face, you remember, and the blow on his head, and the shock, together with the dreadful life he had led in that slum, had completely altered his manner. He didn't stand upright, or look any one in the face when he came to the hospital.'

'He will be quite himself again soon, I hope.'

'Oh, yes! I—I could see a change come over him as soon as he looked at me. As he gets stronger, and his face fills out again it will be difficult to see any difference in him.'

'Well, he will have a devoted nurse!'

'Lots of them! But I shan't be one. He's not in my ward, you know.'

'Perhaps it is just as well for your other patients that he isn't in your ward,' said Great Aunt Julia with a smile.

'Oh, quite!' said Jill.

CHAPTER XIX

VISITORS FOR CYRUS

Jill left Bloomsbury directly after tea, having written a long letter to her father in the afternoon. Miss Lomax made her promise to write a card telling just how she found the patient that evening, and when he would be ready to leave hospital.

'Say I will come and see him to-morrow,' she said. 'I would come to-night if you had not impressed on me the importance of keeping strictly all hospital rules.'

Jill met Dr. Norman on the stairs, and laughed when he said, 'You didn't forget to come back early, I see! I want another look at Mr. Lomax before I let you into the ward, though.'

'I'm glad I saw you, Doctor,' said Jill. 'My aunt is anxious to have my cousin go to stay with her. She wants to know when he will be fit to leave hospital, and if she may come and see him to-morrow.'

'He can have visitors on the usual visiting days now,' said the doctor. 'I am going to tell Sister that his screen can be taken away after you have gone to-night.'

She saw the twinkle in his eye as he spoke.

Jill tried not to blush, but she felt her cheeks grow hot. The doctor went on, 'He can be discharged in a few days, Nurse, as he is to go to friends who will take good care of him. He won't have a long journey, will he?'

'Only to Bloomsbury, Doctor.'

'That will be all right, then. I won't keep you longer than I can help.'

He entered the ward, while Jill stopped to speak to the Sister. The recognition of the unknown patient had greatly interested all the staff, and Jill got a hint that she would be able to slip in every day and see her cousin when she was off duty.

She was very grateful, for she knew that,

as a rule, the nurses were not encouraged to visit other wards.

'Don't let him talk *too* much,' said the doctor, when he came out. 'You can do the talking can't you?'

Jill smiled as she said, 'Yes!' and went into the ward. Cyrus was watching eagerly for her, and told her that the time had passed slowly.

'Why,' said Jill, 'I thought that time didn't bother you a bit.'

'Of course I was impatient to see you again. How is Great Aunt Julia?'

'Quite well; she is coming to see you to-morrow, and she wants you to go to Bloomsbury as soon as you are fit to leave the hospital.'

'When will that be?' asked Cyrus, quite casually, and with no trace of the eagerness which the average hospital patient puts into the question.

'Within a week, from what Dr. Norman was just saying to me,' answered Jill.

'So soon!' said Cyrus, with an expressive look.

'Don't you feel strong enough to go out so soon?' asked Jill, wilfully misunderstanding him.

'I don't want to lose you so soon, little girl,' said Cyrus. 'You will see me every day while I am here, won't you?'

'I'll try to,' said Jill, avoiding his eyes. Jill, of all people, who so seldom failed to look folk in the face!

'She was surprised, of course,' said Cyrus, gently changing the conservation to relieve Jill's embarrassment.

'Great Aunt Julia? Oh, yes, I had quite a job to make her believe that it really was you, and even now, I don't think she will be absolutely certain until she has seen you with her own eyes.'

'Your folk will be surprised, too,' said Cyrus. 'I must write to them, Jill, and apologize for my seeming rudeness. It must have looked very ungrateful to go off without a word.'

'They will understand that it wasn't your fault,' said Jill. 'I wired to Dad as soon as I went out this morning, and I wrote him a long letter this afternoon, so he will have full particulars to-morrow by the first post.'

'Jill thinks of everything,' said Cyrus, patting her hand.

'I haven't told Gwen yet,' said Jill, 'but I shall write to her to-night. And you shall have plenty of notepaper and stamps to-morrow. I've brought you your money, Cousin Cyrus. I thought you would want it for clothes and things.'

Cyrus shook his fist. 'Take it away! I won't look at it!' He shut his eyes tightly as he spoke.

'But you must have some money,' said Jill. 'I meant to help you with it before I knew who you were.'

'That sounds funny! I must think that out for a bit.'

Jill put the envelope containing the notes on the bed, and said, 'Well, my time is up! I'm too good a nurse, I hope, to disobey the doctor's orders.'

Cyrus opened his eyes to say good-bye, and caught sight of the envelope.

'Say, now! That's not the one I put them in!'

'I know it isn't; good-bye,' said Jill, and she ran off before the blush on her cheek betrayed the fact that she had kept the envelope with her name on it, the only scrap of writing that Cyrus had left behind him.

Next morning Cyrus looked out on the life of the ward. It was strange to think that all this orderly routine had gone on while he lay unconscious of it, and that most of the patients who now greeted him cordially, and expressed their pleasure at his progress, had been in the same room all that time.

The morning passed much more quickly than he had expected. He saw nothing of Jill, but one of his nurses brought a message from her when she came back from dinner.

As two o'clock drew near, Cyrus noticed

that a restlessness came over the patients. The clock was closely watched, and contents of lockers were reviewed, while confidences about expected visitors were exchanged between the patients.

The younger ones were obviously divided between delight at having a visitor and anticipation of the little offerings that they expected them to bring. The baby of the ward was hoping for a new 'comic' and a bag of toffee, together with anything else that the good sense of his parent might prompt her to bring. Others hoped for the sight of a friendly face, and were lost to worldly considerations. Cyrus learned a lot about his fellow patients before the door opened to admit the first visitor.

The first anxiety shown by the patients who did not recognize their own friends was to see who else had got visitors. The first comer was a brisk little woman with a basket, who trotted to the far end of the ward with a pleasant smile on her face. Her little boy was

nearly well, and she had just heard that she
would be able to take him home in a few days.

Next came a shy girl, looking about timidly
for her father. This was her first visit to the
hospital, and she had never seen so many sick
people before. She was scared by the size of
the building, and awed by the nurses, but she
forgot all this when she found her father at
last—he had seen her as soon as she passed
the door, but was too weak to call to her—and
started to pour out all the home news and
affectionate messages with which she had
been charged.

By five minutes past some dozen visitors
had arrived. They were the people who had
been waiting at the gate, but some of them
had paused to ask the sister or nurses about
the condition of their friends. Then came the
stragglers, all in a hurry, as being aware that
they had lost some of the precious time that
could be spent at the patient's side.

They all looked poor, but no one came
without some little package, which they laid

on the bed or put into the locker at the patient's request.

About quarter-past there came a slow stately step in the corridor, accompanied by another which seemed to adapt itself to the first one. Cyrus looked up to see Great Aunt Julia escorted by Mr. Lomax himself.

'Great Aunt Julia! This sure is kind of you,' said Cyrus. 'And Mr. Lomax! However did you get here? I am delighted to see you both. Do sit down.'

One of the patients who was allowed to get up brought them chairs, and the two visitors sat down and beamed on their American cousin.

'It *is* Cyrus!' said Miss Lomax, solemnly, after a prolonged scrutiny of his features.

'I rather think so!' he agreed laughingly. 'Jill said you wouldn't believe it until you had seen me with your own eyes. Have you seen her yet, sir?' he asked Mr. Lomax.

'No,' he answered. 'I have only been in London a couple of hours—just in time to lunch with Aunt Julia and bring her here. Jill will be on duty at this time of the day, I understand, but I hope to see her for a few minutes before she goes to her lecture this evening.'

'You came straight up as soon as you got her letter, then,' said Cyrus, 'that was very kind of you. I can't tell you how pleased I am to see you again.'

'You poor fellow!' said Mr. Lomax. 'You have had a dreadful experience. You must come to the farm again as soon as Aunt Julia will spare you, though I know that once she gets you under her roof, she won't let you go in a hurry.'

'Certainly not! He owes me a visit!'

Miss Lomax kept her eye on the invalid as if she had vague misgivings that he might turn back into the broken-down figure that Jill had described to her.

'I hope you will forgive my unceremonious departure,' Cyrus began, but Mr. Lomax held up his hand to stop him.

'Not a word, my dear boy! Not a word! My one regret is that this dreadful misfortune befell you while you were under my roof. I have brought your clothes and papers with me, in your larger case.'

'It's good of you to take so much trouble, sir; I could have managed with the smaller one for a time.'

'But that went when you did,' said Mr. Lomax, 'and your razors and things. From what Jill tells me, you could not have taken them.'

'I took nothing, not even a hat, but those scoundrels must have gone back to the house after they laid me out, and taken what they could lay their hands on.'

'Then they fastened the front door again and left by the scullery window,' said Mr. Lomax. 'A slimly built man might wriggle through there, and the catch shuts up with a smart pull. No doubt they were quite up to any trick of that sort.'

'When Jill saw them, they were just on the

point of clearing off, I suppose,' put in Miss Lomax, 'and you, Cyrus, were lying helpless in the shadow.'

'Something like that,' said Cyrus.

'Well, we shall never know the full particulars,' said Mr. Lomax, 'unless they confess when the police get them, as I hope they will.'

'I don't know that I want them to be run in particularly,' said Cyrus.

'Not from revengeful motives, perhaps,' said Mr. Lomax, 'but such wretches are a danger to society.'

'They might have murdered us all that night,' said Great Aunt Julia.

'I have no doubt that the police will want a statement from you,' said Mr. Lomax. 'The doctor told them about the circumstances under which you came to the hospital.'

'I guess I can't withhold what I know about it,' said Cyrus, 'but it is little enough. All that part between the bang on the head and seeing Jill there is very blank.'

'But tell all that you can,' urged Mr. Lomax, 'the sooner those scoundrels are run to earth the better.'

'They are tough lads, I've no doubt,' said Cyrus, 'but I've no ill-will towards them. In fact, I rather fancy that they have done me a good turn without knowing it.'

He had no chance to explain this mysterious remark, even if he had intended to do so, for Jill came to the door of the ward with a message and forgot all about hospital discipline when she saw her father.

'How good of you, Dad! But I might have known that you would fly up as soon as you heard the news. He's looking heaps better than he was, but he badly wants fattening up, doesn't he?'

'You speak as if he were a goose or a turkey,' said Great Aunt Julia.

'I came by train,' said Mr. Lomax. 'But I certainly lost no time in leaving home.'

'You all tease me,' said Jill. 'You ought to be sorry for me! I shall be scalped if my Ward

Sister finds out that I stopped to gossip to visitors.'

She hurried off, telling her father that she could see him later in the evening, and would see him off if he would stop for the last train.

'She looks fine in uniform,' said Cyrus, who had had to be content with a nod and a smile, for Jill had not stopped to speak to him.

'The first time I have seen her in uniform,' said Mr. Lomax. 'She has got very grown-up, don't you think?'

'Has she?' asked Cyrus. 'She seems just the same to me.'

'There is a difference in her,' said Great Aunt Julia.

'I wish I could have stayed to see you another day,' said Mr. Lomax, as the time came for visitors to leave the ward, 'but I promised Freddie I would not stay the night.'

'I'm not flattered, Cyrus,' said Great Aunt Julia. 'He has not been to see me these thirty years, yet he comes up post-haste to see a distant cousin that he didn't know a year ago!'

'Ah, Great Aunt Julia!' said Cyrus with a laugh, 'if you had done the prodigal son stunt, and turned up under mysterious circumstances in Australia, let us say, he'd have made nothing of going half-way round the world to bring you back! I'm sure he wouldn't!'

'Nothing at all!' said Mr. Lomax, 'and I came straight to you, Aunt; didn't I, now?'

'Only because you were afraid you would never find the hospital!' said Miss Lomax. 'Well, good-bye, Cyrus. I'll come to take you to Bloomsbury as soon as the doctor will let you go.'

'Thanks awfully, both of you! It has done me heaps of good to see you. I shall soon be quite fit.'

'And remember that we shall always be pleased to see you at the farm,' said Mr. Lomax.

'I'll be real glad to come back,' said Cyrus.

CHAPTER XX

A WEDDING PRESENT

Great Aunt Julia came in triumph a week later to take Cyrus to Bloomsbury. He had improved steadily, and was by this time almost himself again.

The police had taken a full statement of all that he could tell them about the attack, but they were too late to lay their hands on 'Flash Jack' or his associates. The parents of the sharp child had removed with that promising young person, much to Cyrus's relief, for he had dreaded the thought of having to see them in order to identify them if he were able to do so.

'We can regard the whole incident as closed, then,' he said to Dr. Norman, when the latter told him that the house from which he had been brought to the hospital was locked up and deserted. 'Well, I am content that it should be so.'

'You are the most forbearing fellow I have ever come across,' said the doctor. 'If I had been treated like that when I was trying to do a fellow a good turn, I should be too wild for words. I ought not to complain, though,' he added, 'for it has meant a most interesting piece of professional experience for me.'

'I am deeply in your debt, Doctor,' said Cyrus. 'I am quite aware of that, and wish that I could find some way of showing my gratitude.'

'Give me permission to publish an account of your case in a book I am writing, and you will leave me infinitely in your debt.'

'Say, now, that's nothing to do at all! You must let me do more than that. Isn't there any fund that I could help here?'

'Dozens of 'em!' said the doctor, 'if you have the means and the inclination. We try to help patients to get to convalescent homes, supply them with crutches and glasses, even with medicine in some cases, after they leave here.'

'I'll send along a cheque,' said Cyrus. 'I hope I shall see something of you while I am in London.'

'Miss Lomax has asked me to call,' said the doctor, 'and I hope to do so. I still take an interest in you, although you are passing out of my charge now.'

'I guess I'll have to look you up after I come back from New York, too,' said Cyrus. 'I'm hoping to want your kind services then.'

'People don't often *hope* to want my services,' said the doctor, 'but you can command them at any time. Go slow for a bit, won't you?'

'I will. Many thanks, and good-bye!'

The hearty grip that Cyrus gave the doctor at parting told how quickly he had regained his strength. The patients watched him go as people in a fairy story might have watched a prince who had cast off a spell and regained his own personality once more. The romance of his story had given him a wonderful interest in their eyes. It was like a fairy tale come true, and it cast a glamour over the dreary hospital days. The tale of the man who lost and recovered his memory was talked about among themselves when there were no visitors to vary the monotony, and was re-told to every visitor for weeks after.

Jill went to Bloomsbury on the evening of the day when Cyrus left the hospital. She had peeped from the window of her own ward to see him go, but he did not know that.

'All alone?' said Jill.

'Yes, Great Aunt Julia has gone upstairs to write some very important letters, and she is not to be disturbed on any account.'

'Oh,' said Jill. Then she wished that she had not answered at all, for the remark sounded so silly, and had the effect of bringing the conversation up with a jerk before it had properly begun.

'Sit down,' said Cyrus.

Jill took a seat near the door without speaking, and looked at her shoes.

'There's plenty of room here,' said Cyrus, who was sitting on the couch. But Jill didn't move so he had to cross the room to fetch her.

He took her hands smilingly, as if he were going to lead her across the room to the couch, but once he had them in his own big ones, the pale hands that had been so brown when he first came to the farm, he forgot all about that, and stood looking at her.

They were divided by the length of both their arms for a time, but Jill found herself gently drawn nearer until her head rested on his shoulder.

'Tell me, Jill, that I'm not mistaken! You do love me?'

'Yes,' said Jill, looking up now, and no longer taking any interest in her shoes. 'But how did you know?'

'Your eyes told me, when you first came round that screen,' said Cyrus. 'I thought I couldn't be mistaken, though you have tried to hide it ever since.'

'You think I'm a forward hussy!' said Jill,

'giving my—love——' (with the slightest pause and a little smile over the word) 'unasked and all that.'

'But not unwanted,' said Cyrus. 'Dear Jill, who could see you and not love you! Now let's talk business!'

They talked 'business' of not too dreary a kind, let us hope, for a good hour, and then Great Aunt Julia coming down from her very important correspondence, wanted to know how they had got on without her.

'Excellently!' said Cyrus, promptly. 'That sounds like an unpardonably rude remark to make to you, Great Aunt Julia, but you'll forgive me, I hope, when I tell you that Jill has promised to be my wife.'

'Of course she has!' said Great Aunt Julia, showing the greatest satisfaction at the news.

Jill went and kissed her. 'But we couldn't have been so happy if Great Aunt Julia hadn't put forward the plan of my coming to the hospital when I did,' she said. 'There haven't been any new pro.'s since I started, so if I hadn't come then, I couldn't have got in at all.'

'And I should have been wandering in the darkness,' said Cyrus, who had heard from the doctor a little about his former state. He came to the other side of the old lady, and put his arm round her shoulder.

'So it's right that we should tell you first,' said Jill, 'though we are both going to write to Dad to-night.'

'When are you going to walk off with her?' asked the old lady, looking fondly at Jill.

'Tell her, Cyrus,' said Jill.

'I want her to quit that old hospital and marry me right away,' said Cyrus.

'A very good plan,' said the old lady.

'No, it isn't!' struck in Jill, forgetting that Cyrus was to do the explaining, 'because that would be like deserting the dear old place, and we both owe so much to it.'

'She's sure it can't be run without her!' teased Cyrus.

'No, it's not that at all—but—Cyrus wants

to—has promised me —— Do go on, dear, you will explain so much better than I can.'

'I'm going to give my litte wife a hospital for a wedding present,' said Cyrus gleefully.

'*A hospital!*'

'Yes, she's that fond of them, that I couldn't get her to cross the Atlantic unless I promised to give her one!'

'Give her the moon!' exclaimed Great Aunt Julia.

'I would have a good shot at that, if Jill wanted it, but I understand she'll be quite content with a little hospital to play about with.'

'A doll's house?' said Great Aunt Julia.

'No, no, a real hospital, for the people in my factory. They really want something of the sort, for accidents and illnesses; and welfare clinics and what not. Jill knows all about it.'

'Not yet,' whispered Jill.

'Well, she will know enough to play with it quite nicely when she has finished her train-

ing, so I have got to wait, but I suppose I
ought to be only too glad to get such a wife
on any terms!'

He really did look quite well satisfied.

'More than two years yet,' Miss Lomax
reminded them.

'Yes, it is a long time,' said Cyrus, 'but
I'm to have a good long holiday here, and
then I shall have to go over and see about the
site and the plans and the equipment and all
the rest of it.'

'And Jill is to be the Matron, I suppose,'
said Great Aunt Julia, 'though how much
you expect to see of your wife under those
conditions, I really do not know.'

'Oh, not a *Matron*!' said Jill in shocked
tones. 'I couldn't be a Matron without being
staff nurse and then sister and then assistant-
matron, and that would take years and years.'

'I can't think of waiting for her to get
through all those stages,' said Cyrus, 'and as
Jill won't hear of having a staff that isn't
properly qualified, we had to compromise.

She is to be a fully-fledged nurse, with certificates and what not, so that she can butt in when she feels like it, and nurse the patients when I am busy, and she has nothing else to do, but we shall have a good staff and we are hoping to get Dr. Norman to take charge.'

'Young man,' said Great Aunt Julia, 'you have been deceiving us!'

'How's that?'

'This scheme will cost money!'

'Oh, yes, but it's to be quite a small place, you know. Jill wants a homey sort of atmosphere, small wards and so on.'

'You did not tell us you were a millionaire!'

'Say, now, I thought you English considered it bad form to talk dollars. I'm not the world's greatest capitalist, by any means, but I guess I can finance the "Julia Lomax Hospital".'

'Is that what you are going to call it?' asked Great Aunt Julia.

'Yes, dear, after both of us, don't you see!' said Jill, softly.

'Well, we do happen to bear that name,' said the old lady with a smile. 'Go on, tell me some more.'

'Cyrus is going to build and equip the hospital,' Jill went on, 'that will be my wedding present. But we don't want the patients to feel that they are accepting charity, so there will be a contributory scheme—quite voluntary, of course. The men will pay a small weekly sum which will entitle them to medical attention for themselves and their families. I hope we shall run a children's ward and a welfare clinic right from the start, and an after-care department to watch cases that have been discharged from the hospital. Then there will be ample provision for research work too, that's where we hope to persuade Dr. Norman to take charge of the hospital, though it will be a small and insignificant post for a man of his standing and ability.'

'He'll have a free hand, though,' said Cyrus. 'I believe we can get him.'

'And when this fairy castle is built, we shall

have to give up our Jill,' said Miss Lomax. 'Once she has that to amuse her, she will never think of England again.'

'Oh, yes, I shall,' said Jill, quickly. 'Cyrus has promised to bring me over every year. And there's not the slightest reason, Great Aunt Julia, why you should not pay us long visits. We should love to have you.'

'We sure should!' said Cyrus.

'You have got through an enormous amount of business in a very short time,' said Great Aunt Julia. 'I don't suppose a scheme like yours ever took shape so quickly before.'

'It's not quite so sudden as you seem to think,' said Cyrus. 'Jill has talked so much about the hospital, that I made up my mind before I came here to give her a little one.'

'It's a kind of thank-offering for what my hospital has done for Cyrus—and for me, too,' explained Jill.

'It's the most delightful wedding present I ever heard of,' said Great Aunt Julia, with something that glistened in her eye. 'Just the thing for Jill, I'm sure! Good luck to your plan. You should be all the happier for this, my dears!'

They were silent for a moment as they thought of the future.

'We've got to talk to Dad, of course,' said Jill, 'but I don't think he will make any objection. He thinks a lot of Cyrus, and we even have hopes of persuading him to come and live with us. Of course, I must have Gwen with me! I shall make my husband build her a school, if she won't come without one!'

They all laughed heartily at this.

'You are good at making plans, Jill!'

'And Cyrus is such a dreadfully competent business man that I can rely on their all being carried out to the letter,' said Jill.

'I shall love doing things for her,' said Cyrus. 'You will be hearing of nothing but plans for the rest of the time I am in England.'

'There's one detail I should like to hear about now,' said Great Aunt Julia.

'What's that?' said Jill and Cyrus together.

'The opening ceremony,' said Miss Lomax.

'That's all arranged, too,' said Jill delightedly. 'We shall be married over here, and the crossing will be our honeymoon trip. We shall arrive just in time to see Miss Julia Lomax open the new building.'

'You mean Mrs. Cyrus J. Lomax,' said Great Aunt Julia with a smile.

'No, I don't! We want you to open it! You will, won't you?'

'There is not much I would refuse you, Jill,' said Great Aunt Julia, 'but on this occasion I feel it would be only fitting to fall back on the family motto, and "Let Jill do it!"'